Abundantly Clear

RACHEL RAFFERTY

Abundantly Clear

Published by Rachel Rafferty 2022

Print Edition

Visit: Rachelrafferty.com

'An Ocean and a Rock'

Lisa Hannigan
(Sea Sew)

Prologue

AS SOON AS the sign was hung on my door, I felt validated. Like a true professional! It read,

'Beatrice Walsh BA MA PhD
University Lecturer
Geography Department'

Everything I'd worked for had come to fruition with the sight of this gold-plated, oblong-shaped wooden sign framed in even-grained mahogany. It fit the space perfectly. I photographed it when no one was looking and sent it to Jeffrey.

He messaged back to say how proud he was of me and that I was on the cusp of showing one of the most prestigious universities in Dublin just what I was made of. I laughed to myself when I read his super-long message that ended with, 'I can't wait to SHOW you just how thrilled I am for you!'

When I got home I reminded him that we had boxes to unpack and furniture to buy for our brand new house. However, the minute I walked in the door, he grabbed me at the waist and kissed me on the lips, as was his way.

After a minute or so, I came up for air. I had to. I stepped back a little.

'Jeffrey, I can't believe I'm finally the professional I've worked so hard to become! All the sacrifices I've made with extra studies and classes have paid off! The sign on my office door says it all. I'm a PROFESSIONAL in my field!'

'I always knew you could do this, Beatrice!'

With that, he kissed me again, softly and slowly. I couldn't believe we were moving in together. How would I get anything done with this gorgeous man kissing me constantly?

I'd made it now, as an individual. And we'd made it as a couple. Both progressing with speed in our respective careers, newly married, ferociously in love and proud owners of a four-bedroomed detached house in one of the most sought-after areas in north County Dublin.

'Thanks for supporting me. I love you,' I replied. The kissing continued and no more moving boxes were unpacked. They could wait. He couldn't. And neither could I.

Chapter One

'IF WE DIDN'T have greenhouse gases, Earth would have an average temperature of approximately -18 degrees celsius. That's clearly not the case...'

I read from my comprehensive notes to a lecture hall of seemingly disinterested, hungover students. I tried my best to make it sound interesting, using pacing and intonation, but it didn't work. They continued sending text messages and doodling or yawning without covering their mouths. Some were doing all three, showing no awareness of how it made me feel. I carried on regardless, willing the bell to ring. I noticed that if I paused between sentences, fifty percent of the heads would look up and I could hold their attention for a short period. It wasn't long before they sussed out that I was only doing it for that very reason. I changed tack and began pausing mid sentence, sometimes for up to ten seconds. That worked for a few lectures, although the facts got a bit disjointed. Even I got mixed up as my mind wandered during the long pause. I occasionally lost where I was and accidentally finished off the sentence with an alternative fact.

This happened at my mid-morning lecture on Thursday in University College North Dublin, also known as UCND.

'The theory of plate tectonics states that the Earth's solid outer crust, the lithosphere, is separated...'—pause ... approx 10 seconds—'...em, these hardened mounds of lava, called pillow lavas, have been pushed up and are now visible at the surface.'

Wait a sec, did I just...? Was that a different paragraph? When I looked up, I realised the students appeared just as confused as me. Hah! So they were listening after all! I caught them!

'Okay, go through the PowerPoint presentation and we'll pick up again on Tuesday,' I concluded the lecture, acknowledging their raised eyebrows and baffled expressions. *Well, it's not my fault I'm forced to find creative ways to maintain attention, is it?* I collected my notes and books in order to leave the lecture hall, amid the hustle and bustle of students scurrying to the canteen. I phoned Jeffrey on my way to the staff cafeteria.

'Well, how was he this morning?'

'Oh, I'm fine thanks, darling. How are you?'

'Jeffrey, come on. Tell me.'

'He was grand. I dropped him off before the

school run and they were delighted to see him back at creche.'

'Did they take his temperature?'

'No, but I told them I did and it was grand.'

'Oh, what was it?'

'Bang on 37.'

'Oh good. And did the girls get to school on time?'

'Yes, all under control, now go and have your break!'

I was better able to enjoy my lunch knowing that Daniel, my youngest, was safe and well in playschool. It was such a relief that Jeffrey could be at the school within ten minutes to collect the children if they were sick. The joys of having one parent working from home.

As I sat down to eat, Mr. Keel's assistant from the geography department joined me.

'Hi Beatrice, I think I mentioned this to you before? The rock study in the west of Ireland. I have a contact for you. He's a local fisherman, called Henry McCormack. Is it okay to give him your number to organise an excursion?'

'Oh, that was quick!'

'Yeah, the most westerly townland has a very small population, so everyone knows everyone. A few people mentioned Henry and told me he'd have the time to dedicate to the project.'

'Very good. Does he have much local

knowledge?'

'Born and bred in Glan Mahogue. I had a chat with him and from what I can gather there's nothing he doesn't know about the local rock formations, flora and fauna. You name it, he had something to say on everything. To be honest, you'll have a hard time getting him off the phone.'

'Oh, okay, well thanks for the heads up.'

'And, one more thing, he has quite a strong, west of Ireland accent, paired with a lisp. The more he talks, the more your ears become attuned to it. Just thought you should be aware of that ahead of making contact.'

'Well, thanks again for the warning. I'll go somewhere quiet with no background noise, so I can concentrate.'

'Good thinking. Okay, Beatrice, here are his details and best of luck with the project. Keep me updated. And, em, I believe Mr. Keel wants to speak with you soon, so you can keep him informed also.'

'He does? Of course, thanks, I will.'

Hmmm, Henry McCormack. I was starting to get excited about my rock study and upcoming trip out west. My phone alarm sounded, telling me it was time for my next lecture. Oh no, first years... Uhhhh.

✧ ✧ ✧

WHEN I ARRIVED at the lecture theatre, there were less than 20% of my students present. I stood and waited for more to arrive, but only one straggler drifted in late. With a heavy heart, I launched into my climate control action plan. I'd put so much work into this and I'd really hoped for a fuller lecture hall, but I suppose first years had better things to do with their time. Maybe they were lounging by the lake, meeting for coffee, catching up on Netflix or, most likely, still sleeping off the night before. University was still a novelty for them, their first taste of freedom, and news of their late night parties spread around the campus like wildfire.

When my presentation was finished, I knocked on my hard, wooden table loudly, in order to wake up the two young men in the front row. They didn't look at all familiar to me and I wondered if they'd possibly fallen asleep at the previous lecture on Greek and Roman Civilization, and hadn't gotten a chance to leave the lecture hall yet. They seemed startled when they awoke and looked equally as baffled to see me as I was them. I looked around at the rest of the group, who were smirking or already leaving. I tried to get their attention and let them know I hoped to see more attendees at next week's lecture. I requested that they spread the word amongst their peers. One girl smiled and nodded politely on her way out. It gave me comfort that at least one person had acknowledged my request.

I made a mental note to check with the dean of the geography department about required numbers in the lecture hall. I wondered if there was a minimum number of attendees to warrant cancelling the session. I probably should have rescheduled that one. There was so much valuable information in it that I wanted to impart to my students. I suppose I could repeat it next week anyway, word for word. Would any of them cotton on? With that thought, I grabbed my phone and headphones and went for a walk around the lake at the university campus.

Annoyingly, as soon as Axel Rose started whistling the intro to 'Patience', my phone beeped. Jeffrey was texting about dinner. He was at the shops.

> Jeffrey
> Hey Bea, I know you're busy, but if you get this, give me a thumbs up or down. Fillet steak, fried onions and french red for us. I'll make chicken goujons for the kids. Roasted butternut squash and spuds on the side. Sounds good? Or do you feel like white wine? I can get chicken for us instead?

I raised my eyes. His texts were always ridiculously long winded and detailed. I sent back a thumbs up and replayed the music. Not for long, though. Another beep sounded.

Jeffrey
Is that a thumbs up for chicken? Or the steak? I need more clarity x

Beatrice
Red wine for us. Chicken for kids. Thanks. Having a day of it... you know what I mean x

Jeffrey
Well, hopefully some steak and wine will improve your day! Got salmon for tomorrow. I'll make teriyaki sauce. Or would you prefer garlic butter with it?

Beatrice
Sounds great! I'm walking x

Jeffrey
Again, love, you didn't answer my question. Which will I go for?

Ten minutes later...

Jeffrey
Beatrice?

Five minutes later...

Jeffrey
I'm at the till. Need to pay now. Which sauce?

Beatrice
Oh, have I not made myself clear? Teriyaki please x

✧ ✧ ✧

MY FINAL LECTURE of the day was equally as unsuccessful as the morning ones. And these were third years—*I mean, come on!* The apathy emanating from my students never ceased to amaze me.

'The Plan identifies four strategic priorities to guide implementation. The first is awareness, the second is participation, to provide stakeholders opportunities to engage and contribute to follow-up and review processes, and further develop national enactment of the goals.'

The bell sounded.

'Oh, is that the time?' I was surprised. That flew. 'Okay, review this topic for next week, please. Thank you.'

Well, well, well, I was dumbfounded. To my utter amazement, I spotted a raised hand.

'Yes?' I blurted.

'Oh, em, well, you said the plan identifies four priorities, but you only mentioned two of them. I just wondered...'

'Wondered? Wondered what?'

'Well, what were the other two?'

'I mentioned two, didn't I?' I stuck my head in my notes and leafed through the last few pages. Yes, I did. I mentioned two. When I looked up, the young man who asked the question shrugged and left the lecture hall. I shrugged too. I didn't know what he was asking me. I thought I'd made myself abundantly clear. I shrugged again and as my shoulders fell, I relaxed and felt overwhelming relief that my day at uni was over.

✧ ✧ ✧

WHEN I ARRIVED home that evening, Jeffrey had fed the kids and was plating up our dinner. My face lit up when I eyed the perfectly cooked medium rare steaks we were having. And the smell of the onions caramelising, ooohhhh.

'You're an angel,' I told him, planting a kiss on his lips.

The kids gave me hugs and I asked them how school was. 'Great!' they all shouted, one after the other. Then I enquired what they did in school and each of them supplied me with the same response—

'Nothing!'

'Oh, well, that IS great!' I laughed and let them go into the playroom to watch their programmes.

Jeffrey chuckled too and poured a glass of wine for me.

'How was the rest of your day?'

'Diabolical,' I answered.

'Oh no! Why?'

I just shook my head in despair.

'Really? Was it that bad?' He sounded sympathetic. 'I can understand the first years having no regard. They'll probably drop geography at the end of the year. But the third years? I mean, surely they're showing interest, no?'

'Well, they've a funny way of showing it. That said, I did get one raised hand asking a question.'

'Well then, they ARE interested in your lectures. That proves it.'

'Ah, he was just being smart, asking me to repeat myself.'

'Oh, is that all? So, it wasn't a genuine question, then?'

'Em, well, come to think of it, I can't actually remember what he asked me.'

'Really? Beatrice? The first raised hand and you didn't listen to the question?'

'Jeffrey, just because you happen to be naturally amazing at your job without putting much effort in doesn't mean it happens that way for everyone. I spend copious hours perfecting and preparing material for my lectures and it's hugely disheartening to deliver my impeccable research to a less than half-full lecture hall, where the students are lethargic and disinterested. Most of them look as if all they need is a good night's sleep.'

'Beatrice, steady on! I'm not having a go. I know your job isn't easy. All I'm saying is that if you have an eager student who raises his hand, the least you can do is listen to them. Now, I've said my piece. Would you like a top up?'

'Yes, that wine is delicious. Everything is, actually.'

'I'll do bedtime tonight. You seem tired.'

'Great, thanks. I might just finish this and then have an early night. It would be nice to wake up with a clear head in the morning.'

'Good call!' Jeffrey went to get the kids and bring them to bed. He left his phone on the kitchen counter. He usually had it tucked safely in his back pocket, but he'd just had half a bottle of wine and maybe our conversation distracted him. I was tempted to check it. I knew his code to switch it on. He'd be busy with bedtime for the next 45 minutes. Plenty of time for me to scroll through. I swallowed more wine, while I thought about it. God, it was good. Jeffrey was adept at choosing the exact wine to match a dish. He never let me down. Well, almost never…

I took a few deep breaths, as memories flooded back. Flashbacks of one epic letdown made my eyes water and chest tighten. I wondered if he still kept in touch with her. He'd assured me it was over and I told him I believed him. That was almost a year ago now. Yet, I was still doubting him. I jumped when his phone beeped. Could that be her? Was she still texting him? Flirting with him? I finished the last of my wine and concentrated hard on glueing myself to my seat. I pinned my hands under my buttocks to stay rooted on my chair. It took all of my self-control to stop myself reaching for his phone to have a quick peek. As I sat there, taking slow, even, deep breaths, Jeffrey reappeared in the kitchen.

'Ah, that's where it is! Thought I heard a ding. Will I open another bottle for you, Bea?'

'Hmm? Oh, no thanks. I was just getting up to load the dishwasher. Still thinking about that early night.'

'Yeah, of course. It would do you good.' He approached, pecked me on the cheek and walked out again. Back upstairs to the chaos of bedtime, with his phone firmly tucked into the back pocket of his jeans.

Chapter Two

'HELLO, BEATRICE WALSH here. Is this Henry McCormack I'm speaking to?'

'It is. Oh, Beatrish, it's great to hear your voice.'

'It's Beatrice. Yes, I wanted to discuss the rock study of the western shores with you. Is now a good time?'

'Any time is a good time, Beatrish. I have all the time in the world.'

'Oh, good, that's good. It's, em, BeatriCE, by the way. Right, I'm going to email you a list of questions on the local rock formations and I'm requesting photos too. What kind of camera do you have?'

'Oh Beatrish, I think it would be better if you came to visit me and saw the beach for yourself. A photo won't do it justice and I'm no photographer. When can you come?'

'Well, I was planning a visit closer to the summertime actually, but...'

'Why put it off? I could be dead by then.'

'Really? Is there an underlying issue I don't know about?'

'Make hay while the sun shines, Beatrish.'

'Oh. Oh yes, I've heard that one before. Look, I'll check with Mr. Keel regarding organising a field trip. Maybe you're right. The sooner I see it for myself, the better I'll know what direction the project should take.'

'I'll be ready and waiting for you, Beatrish. I'm looking forward to it already.'

'You are? Okay, thanks Mr. McCormack, I'll...'

'Henry.'

'Thanks, Henry.'

Wow! He seems keen, I thought, as I headed to Lecture Hall 4 for my second years. Oh, drat, the second years, they were so...I don't know, bleh. Yes, bleh, that was the only way to describe them really. *Why me? Why do I put myself through this?*

Suddenly, my phone beeped. It was a photo of Glan Mahogue beach, sent by Henry. He was quick off the mark. Top marks for gusto, I credited him with that much, and the beach was nothing short of breathtaking. Now, THAT was why I put myself through this—I smiled at the apt reminder. It was my love of geography, of course! The natural. The ruggedness. The grey, hard, smooth rock. The sight of the seaweed-stained rock in the photo was enough to get me aroused, ever so slightly. I was in the university corridor, but I stopped in my tracks and gulped, reaching my hand out to caress the cold, concrete of the 80 year old wall by my side. I took some deep breaths, as the iciness of the wall penetrated my fingers. One thing I knew for sure was that I wanted to get myself to Glan Mahogue as soon as possible to caress that jagged limestone and straddle those seaborne rock formations. I took a quick detour to the bathroom to pull myself together, before greeting the second year sods.

They sat there, wide eyed, no doubt feigning their enthusiasm. They were better attendees than the first years and more interested than the third years, but I saw right through them. I sensed quantity over quality the minute I launched into my lecture.

'Supporting evidence for the idea came from the dove-tailing outlines of South America's east coast and Africa's west coast, and from the matching of the rock formations along these edges.'

'Excuse me?'

'Who said that?' I jumped in fright.

'Eh, me, Ms. Walsh, over here.'

'Yes? Is there a problem?'

'I just wondered about the supporting evidence, I...'

'Yes, I'm pretty sure I explained that. Anything

else?'

'Oh, well, I was going to ask if...'

'What did you say your name was?'

'Oh, I didn't. It's Karl. I just had a question about...'

'Karl, would you mind awfully if I asked you to email me your question later? It's just that your interruption is disturbing my flow and I've so much that I want to get through today. Is that okay, Karl? Would you mind?'

Ah, that was better. Now I could carry on pouring out my geography knowledge without any interruptions. It would be disjointed if I kept stopping mid lecture to answer questions. In this way, I could make my output abundantly clear.

✧ ✧ ✧

I QUICKLY MADE an appointment with Mr. Keel, the dean of the department, to discuss departing on my field trip sooner rather than later. He sounded very eager to talk to me and told me to come to his office that same afternoon. In the meantime, I Googled the westerly point of Glan Mahogue, and it became apparent to me why it was chosen as the destination of the rock study. It was untouched and wild. It had been allowed to morph naturally without outside interference. A hidden gem. I also checked and rechecked my lecture notes and corrections and ensured all my planning was up to date, before my meeting with Mr. Keel. I knew he'd asked a few other staff members to pull up their socks when it came to lecture planning, although my notes were of such a high calibre, I couldn't fathom he'd have any complaints about them. I entered his office at five o'clock, thinking I'd be out and on the road home in a jiffy. Turns out I was wrong.

He smiled when I walked into his office. Oh, how I loved his office! Landscapes of jagged countryside and deserted beaches filled the wall space behind him and there was a personal story to go with each and every photograph. My favourite was the one he'd taken thirty years ago of himself and his then fiancée at Coumeenole beach in Co Kerry. They had the beach to themselves and the wildness of the waves paired powerfully with the fire in his fiancée's eyes. He even managed to capture the multi-layered evening sunset with his masterful photography. That photo stunned me and every time I entered his office, I became mesmerised by it.

'Beatrice, I'm glad you contacted me. I've been meaning to arrange a meeting with you.'

'Oh, I brought my lecture notes with me. Here, I'll just fire up my laptop now.'

'No, that's not why I wanted to see you, Beatrice. I have full confidence in your planning and preparation for lectures. It's…it's, oh, this is more difficult than I imagined. You know I respect your dedication and your research. You're an esteemed and valued member of this department.'

'Mr. Keel, please, say what you want to say.'

'Yes, yes, you're quite right. I'll get to the point, Beatrice.' He paused, before continuing. 'It's your delivery. That is the issue.'

'My delivery?' *What's he talking about? I'm not a postman.*

'Yes, the way you impart your informed knowledge to the students.'

'I don't understand, Mr. Keel. My research and lecture notes are of the highest standard and I can guarantee you that…'

'Please, Beatrice, you're missing the point. The problem is the way you communicate with the students.'

'Pardon me? I think I make myself abundantly clear!'

'No, no, well, I'm sure it's clear to you, but I'm afraid it isn't to your students.'

'What…what do you mean? How do you know this?'

'There have been complaints, Beatrice. Complaints made to me about the delivery of your lectures. Please understand, I'm just the messenger. I can't let this go, I need to address the concerns of our geography students.'

'Oh? What kind of complaint did you receive?'

'Okay, well, here's one of them—'Ms Walsh begins to explain something, but trails off and ends her sentence with something entirely different. It doesn't make sense.' And...'

'Well, we have to allow for human error every now and then, don't we?' I offered, with a wide-eyed innocent shrug.

'Ahem, here's another—'Ms Walsh is very unapproachable.' And'

'It's not my fault if a student doesn't have the neck to approach me.'

'One more—'Ms Walsh refuses to answer questions at the end of lectures.' Would you like me to continue?'

'You mean there's more?' I enquired with a dwindling sense of nonchalance.

'Afraid so.'

'How many more?'

'Emm, one sec.' He reached for a folder on his desk with printouts and handwritten notes stapled together. Each bunch had a sticky note on the front, stating what date it was that the complaints were received. Oh no, I thought, there were enough to organise and file. I began to wish I hadn't asked.

'Well, Beatrice, as you can see. I've printed and kept all feedback from the students over the past few months. Usually, if there's a small number, we tend to either ignore it, or speak to the individual students and encourage them to approach the lecturer. But, em, for some reason, your students don't feel comfortable approaching you. It's like they don't want to hurt your feelings. And then, they come to me with their concerns and to be quite honest, it has come to the point now where I simply have to take action.'

'Oh. Oh, I see.' Was he going to fire me? *Please, ground, swallow me up—now.*

'We need to address this, Beatrice. You do understand, don't you?'

'Address it? How?'

'Well, it seems clear that your current regime is not functioning in a satisfactory way. The students are reluctant to ask you questions, even in the tutorials, where there are smaller numbers.'

'Are they? I thought they just weren't interested. They don't look as if they're even listening.'

'Yes, I know what you mean, but obviously some of them are. Enough to make these formal complaints.'

'I...I just don't get it. My notes are meticulous. I've worked so hard on them and update them regularly with new information. I mean, I never stop. You've seen me in the library and...'

'Yes, Beatrice, I have and I don't doubt your commitment for one second. I think you're just falling short with communicating your knowledge to your students.'

Silence followed. I just had to let it all sink in. He continued.

'Your content is second to none. I know how many hours you spend compiling your research, but I'm afraid the students don't feel as if they're benefitting from it, and if that's the case, I suppose, what's the point?'

I looked down at my hands on my lap and started twisting my wedding ring around and around. He was going to fire me. Oh my God, Mr. Keel, who I respected more than anyone in the world, was going to fire me. My hands were getting sweaty due to my fingers expanding, so my ring wouldn't turn anymore.

'Might I suggest something, Beatrice?'

'Hmm?' I looked up. 'Yes, yes of course.'

'I'd like to recommend that you take a course in communications. There's a part-time course starting in two weeks on campus. Just one or two evenings a week as far as I know. I can't remember the schedule as such, but I'll email you the link later. Is that something you might consider?'

'Yes, yes it is, if you think it's necessary.'

'Oh, great. I can inform the students that their complaints are being addressed in a proactive way. That's marvellous! Thanks for taking this so well, Beatrice.'

'So, a communication's course?'

'Yes, it should help you impart your valuable knowledge with more clarity. Does that make sense?'

'Hmm? Oh yes, yes it does. More clarity is what I need.' I was just so relieved he didn't give me the chop. And, so grateful. Oh, Mr. Keel, thank you, I beamed inwardly.

'Indeed. And, it will assist with your delivery too. Is that all okay? As I said, I'll send you on the details later this evening.'

'That sounds like a plan, Mr. Keel. And a perfectly reasonable one at that!'

✧ ✧ ✧

BY THE TIME I got home that evening, I'd received three more messages from that Henry McCormack, but I ignored all of them. I just wanted to recount the events of the day with Jeffrey. However, he was busy being 'Super Dad' and putting the kids to bed, so it gave me time to check the emails that Mr. Keel sent. When I read the course outline, I found myself getting oddly excited about embarking on something new. I never imagined I'd be further developing my skills in my midlife. At forty years of age, I assumed I'd be on the wind down, with early retirement options firmly in sight. But, no, with this new course I'd be broadening my horizons, upskilling and becoming a master of my trade. Jeffrey was in shock when I shared the news.

'What? A communications course? How will you even have time for that?'

'Look, Jeffrey, I'll just have to make the time, if I want to keep my job.'

'So, it's that serious, is it?'

'It is, Jeffrey, it really is. Mr. Keel wants me to do this course to improve my lecture delivery. He made his point and he made it abundantly clear.'

Chapter Three

THE WEEKEND CAME at last. Jeffrey brought the kids to visit Granny and Grandad, so I had the house to myself for a couple of hours. I opened the messages from Henry McCormack. He was selling himself short regarding his lack of photography skills. The images he sent were clear as day and professionally cropped. Close-ups of crystals on metamorphic rock, stretches of green, grassy cliff tops and panoramics of long, stoney beaches. I was blown away by the scope of it all. Being a fisherman, he was out at sea bright and early. Therefore he had breathtaking images of the golden sky at dawn. The romance of it all captured my heart and I found myself matching Henry's enthusiasm about my impending visit.

Beatrice
Two weeks, Henry, I promise I'll be there in two weeks from now!

Henry
Oh Beatrish, you'll come out on the boat

with me, won't you? At the crack of dawn, we'll sail west and catch a fish or two for our lunch.

Beatrice
Wow! That sounds amazing! I've never gone fishing before.

Henry
Can you swim, Beatrish?

Beatrice
Not very well, Henry. You'll have to dive in and save me if I fall overboard! LOL!

No response. Oh, I guess he didn't think that was funny. Was it unprofessional of me to make a joke with him? Or, doesn't he have a sense of humour? Still no response. Oh well...

I got back to researching my new course in communication. It was due to start on Tuesday evening. I began to get excited about it when I explored the course content. I got flashbacks of things I'd learned in teacher training college twenty years ago. Back when I thought I wanted to be a secondary school teacher. Before I'd laid eyes on Jeffrey. It was him who encouraged me to propel my career into third level. He saw my passion for geography and spurred me on to study a master's degree in my beloved subject. He supported me in every step of my career transition, but I barely had a chance to settle in before I got pregnant with the twins. I'd only been lecturing for six months when I had to go on early maternity leave.

The shock of having twins nearly killed us, but we muddled through somehow with the help of grandparents. I found it hard to find my footing after that in the geography department. My so-called mentor was on maternity leave and I was left to fend for myself as a newbie. A subsequent pregnancy with Daniel pulled me right back to square one, but Jeffrey had my back, professionally speaking.

He was so career driven, it was infectious. Had I not bothered with the master's degree, I probably would have settled into a nice, cushy number as a secondary school teacher in north County Dublin. Maybe I would have taken a career break and become a stay-at-home mom, but because I was starting out in third level, I felt I needed to push forward and try to make my family life fit in somehow. Everything could and would have gone swimmingly, if Jeffrey hadn't gotten involved with someone else.

I wish I'd never seen her. I wish I didn't know what she looked like. I wish I didn't know that she was younger, prettier and blonder than me. Probably brainier also—I knew she was a doctor. I was reminded of a time when my mother took me aside a few weeks before my wedding day—

'Beatrice, you know we love Jeffrey and he's crazy about you, but are you sure, really sure, you want to do this?'

'Mam! What are you talking about? Why would you ask me that?'

'It's just that me and your dad were talking and, em, as you know, Jeffrey is very good looking, VERY good looking and...well, women will just fall at his feet. Will you be able to handle that? All that female attention he gets?'

I was disgusted with her at the time and fobbed her off, but it turns out, there was substance to her words. Jeffrey did get a lot of female attention. Even the nurses and midwives, both male and female, were fussing over him, when I was panting at seven centimetres about to give birth to twins. As for him, he always laughed it off and reassured me that I was the one for him.

Until I wasn't. Until I wasn't enough for him, or he got distracted by Linda's charms. I mean it beggars belief how someone could end up falling for their doctor and having an affair with them. At that moment, my phone beeped.

Henry
Neither can I.

Beatrice
Sorry Henry??

Henry
I can't swim either.

Beatrice
Really? You're a fisherman! You're at sea every day!

Henry
Yeah. I live life on the edge.

Gulp. Oooh, this guy was getting to me now. He was very full on and flirtatious. My phone beeped again. This time it was a picture of him. Fwahhh! He was on his boat, sailing into the sunset with a glint in his eye. He was beautiful. He blended in with the landscape around him—rugged, earthy, raw. The colour of his eyes matched the sea and the cheekiness in his grin did something to me. Fwahhh! I didn't look again at my communications course content, but rather focussed on Henry's image instead. I had the house to myself so I took my phone upstairs, undressed and crawled into bed. *Got to make the most of these moments at my age.*

Myself and Jeffrey were more companions now than lovers since his affair. We really loved and respected each other, but I was so hurt by his indiscretion and he felt so guilty apparently, that we never got back to where we were. We didn't know how to make that leap. But, I still had desire. And imagination. And, now this. I perched my phone upright on my bedside locker, so the image of Henry McCormack lit up the screen. It seemed as though his piercing sea-blue eyes were staring right through me. And I kind of wished they were.

✧ ✧ ✧

'YOU'RE IN A good mood!' Jeffrey noticed when he got home.

'Well, I had peace and quiet all afternoon. It was blissful. Thanks for that. What's in the bags?' I enquired.

'Oh. These? I just, em, nipped to the shops while the kids were playing mini golf with Grandad.'

'Oh? You didn't stay with them?'

'No, no, they were fine. Yeah, I, eh, just needed a few things.'

I looked expectant, so he continued.

'Yeah, just t-shirts, socks and toiletries. You know yourself.'

'Looks like you did quite the stock up. You know if you're running low on anything, I can pick up stuff on my way home from work, especially on Thursdays, when the shops are open late.'

'Not anymore, you can't!'

'Hmmm? What do you mean?'

'Isn't your communications course on every Tuesday and Thursday evening?'

'Oh, goodness, yeah, I almost forgot.'

'Forgot? I thought that's what you were working on all afternoon?' He looked confused.

'Yeah, I did. I looked into it, a little bit anyway. I'm excited to start on Tuesday!'

With that, Jeffrey changed the subject. 'Here, look, prosecco! Will I open it? Mum won it at bingo last week and she doesn't like the sparkly stuff. "Just for kids", she said.'

'Hah! Did she say that? Yeah, it looks good. I'll have a glass,' I replied.

'Yeah, me too. I'll just put these bags away and whip up a quick salad for us. The kids ate already. I'll stick this bottle in the freezer. It's not as cold as it should be.'

✧ ✧ ✧

I HARDLY SLEPT a wink on Monday night, being so angst ridden ahead of my new venture into communications. I tossed and turned wondering if I'd be the oldest in the class or if they'd all be media students. I also worried that I might recognise someone, or worse still, they'd recognise me. A past pupil maybe, or something awkward like that. I was keeping the fact that I was embarking on further education between me, Jeffrey and the grandparents. We might need the folks for babysitting if Jeffrey had a late meeting and couldn't collect the kids. Of course, they immediately wondered if I was chasing a career change, so I had to embarrassingly admit that it was recommended to me to upskill in order to keep the career I had. They noticed my discomfort and we said no more about it, apart from them wishing me the best of luck.

My trip out west would have to wait a little longer too. I wanted to settle into my course before beginning the rock study project. Henry was very disappointed when I texted to let him know. He rang me.

'Ah Beatrish, I have everything ready for you. I thought you were coming next week?'

'I know, Henry, but I've had to change my plans. You know, I have a family and a husba—'

'Ah, now, let's not get personal, Beatrish. Your business is your business and mine is mine.'

'Oh, well, right, so you understand. Do you have a family, Henry?'

'No, Beatrish. I'm saving myself for the right woman. I just haven't met her yet.'

'Oh, okay, well as you said, let's not get personal.'

'No, not until you get here anyway.'

What does that mean? He puzzled me a lot. Was he flirting or was this just his way? I couldn't figure him out. I ended the call as I had to get to work. I was about to get in my car when I realised it was Tuesday—bin day. Jeffrey forgot again.

What had gotten into him lately? He was constantly engrossed in his phone or laptop, even though he told me things were quiet at work. I went to roll the wheelie bin out to the verge. Oh, it seemed light. Maybe he didn't put it out on purpose. I opened the lid to check. Ah, it was three-quarters full. That warranted collection, in my opinion.

As I was walking back to the car, something niggled at me. Was that a…? Did I just see a bag from… Hang on. I returned to the bin to look inside again. I was right. A bag within a bag. I pulled it out. The red and white stripes were eye-catching, but Jeffrey had squashed it into another bag. An attempt to hide it, maybe? It was from *Bella Mae Luxury Skincare*. I recognised it because Margaret, my mother-in-law, had given me a gift from there last Christmas. A twin lipstick set, packaged in a red and white striped bag, tied with red ribbons. I loved it so much that I'd kept the bag. What was Jeffrey buying there? My birthday had already passed, so who was he surprising? My head started to hurt. The sleepless night paired with the shock of this. What was going on? I got into my car and reached for the glove compartment where I found painkillers. I needed something to stop the ache. I couldn't ring in sick either. Not today. Mr. Keel had made it abundantly clear how important it was for me to do this communications course. My career depended on it.

Chapter Four

'BEING A GOOD listener is one of the best ways to be a good communicator. No one likes communicating with someone who doesn't take the time to listen to the other person. Take the time to practise active listening. Active listening involves paying close attention to what the other person is saying, asking clarifying questions such as 'So, what you're saying is...' Through active listening, you will find it easier to respond appropriately.'

Hmmm, I listened attentively to the facilitator and the course content was making sense to me. It hit home. Every word that came out of her mouth resonated with me. I sat back and took it all in. Anxious thoughts of what Jeffrey was getting up to behind my back melted away, and I knew I was in the right place at the right time doing the right thing.

When I got home that evening, Jeffrey had put the kids to bed and was in his office, seemingly deep in concentration. He popped his head through the door.

'Oh! You're home! Hang on, I'll finish up here and come into the kitchen. There's lasagne in the oven. It should still be hot.'

I wondered what had him working late tonight. He usually tells me all about the projects he's working on, but he didn't share anything about this one. The lasagne was still hot, like he said, and just as I was about to tuck in, Jeffrey appeared offering me wine.

'Oh, yes please! I love that one!'

'Yeah, why not? To celebrate the first evening of your course!' He poured a glass for me and a second one for himself. 'So, tell me, how was it?'

'It was...it was brilliant, actually! I mean, so much of it was common sense or techniques I'd learned before in teacher training college, but it's good, so good in fact, to get a reminder of the optimal way to do things.'

'Yeah? Like what?' he asked.

'Well, even just basic listening skills and attuning your brain into actively conversing with someone. Like, for example, if you were to open up and tell me something right now, I, as the listener, would make you feel like you had the floor. I'd give you my full attention and acknowledge everything you said with my eye contact and facial expression.'

I noticed he shifted uncomfortably on his chair

and knocked back a larger than necessary gulp of wine. He rubbed his forehead and muttered something like, 'great, excellent, well done, Beatrice.' Something inconsequential like that. He seemed aware that I was examining him. I hadn't meant to cause tension or accuse him of anything. I really was just relaying some of the course content to him. He looked as though he was sorry he asked. Then, my phone beeped as soon as the last morsel of lasagne was consumed. That was when Jeffrey got up and said he should check on the kids.

'Really? There's not a peep out of them. You might only disturb them if you go in.'

'Ah well, I'll let you check your message. It might be something important from your course. Then, his phone started binging too, so he left. I knew exactly who was messaging me.

Henry
There's a lovely photo of you on the UCND website. I looked up the geography department.

Beatrice
Were you looking for something in particular, Henry? Can I help you with anything?

Henry
I found it, thanks

Was he just messing with me? I mean, he was my contact for a geography project in uni. He was becoming so familiar. I didn't know whether I liked it or found it creepy. I honestly couldn't choose.

Beatrice
Okay, well, Henry, it looks like I'll be heading west in two weeks. My accommodation is being arranged for me.

Henry
No need. I'll sort you out.

Hmmm, sounds ominous. Thrilling or scary, though? I didn't know.

Beatrice
What do you mean?

Henry
I know the perfect location for your stay. I'm sending a photo of your view now.

Oooh. Thrilling! I decided it was thrilling. He sent the photo.

Beatrice
OMG Henry! That is exquisite! How can the hotel be so close to the beach? Yes, book me in there!

'Who's that?'

I jumped out of my seat in fright. I didn't realise Jeffrey had returned.

'What? Hmmm?'

'Oh, sorry. I didn't mean to frighten you. It's just, you looked so happy. I was wondering who you were texting.'

'Oh. Oh yeah, it's nothing,' I answered, but he raised his eyebrows, quizzically.

'Oh well, it's just ...Cara.'

'Cara Cawley? You haven't heard from her in a while, have you?'

'No. So, you know, it's great to hear from her again. That's why I was smiling.'

He nodded and smiled too, deeming my response a perfectly reasonable one. Why did I lie to him? I could have told him it was my project contact in the west of Ireland showing me where I'd be staying on location. Why didn't I just tell him that? My heart rate quickened when I really thought about it. I guess Henry McCormack was becoming my guilty pleasure of late. It's just he always sounded so keen and enthusiastic and he was getting me excited. Not only about the project, but he was rekindling my love of all things rock. With that thought and a sneaky peek at Henry's image, I went off to bed a happy camper after my initial rocky start to the day.

✧ ✧ ✧

AT MY SECOND class on Thursday, they discussed the importance of body language, eye contact and tone of voice. I listened intently.

'A relaxed, open stance and a friendly tone will make you appear approachable and will encourage others to speak openly with you.'

Hmmm, I thought about my awkward stance at my lectures, always struggling to keep my eyes on my notes rather than on my audience. This was something I could definitely work on.

When I arrived home that evening, I refused the wine Jeffrey offered, stating that I wanted to be fresh and clearheaded for my lectures the next morning. I went upstairs to the full-length mirror in our bedroom and practised some relaxed, open stances.

I had to admit I was generally quite rigid in my demeanour at lectures and I supposed it could be a little off-putting for the students. I tried one hand on my hip with my legs a foot apart. Maybe this could be a goer. Hmmm, fairly casual, I thought. Then I tried leaning with one hand resting on a chest of drawers. Nah, too forced. Thirdly, I tried one foot slightly forward, combined with hand movements. Subtle gestures at first, but as I rattled off some course material to the mirror, I found that my facial expression lit up and became more engaging. My hand gestures became more animated. Too animated? I didn't want to appear too keen, too soon. Okay, now to find some middle ground...

I got interrupted. I usually do, in a house of five. This time, not even one of the kids. It was my phone.

Henry
I got your accommodation sorted for you

Beatrice
In that place with the amazing view?

Henry
Yes

Beatrice
Brilliant! I can't wait! Thanks Henry!

I let out an excited squeal.

'Good news?'

'Ahhhhh!' I turned around to find Jeffrey at the doorway.

'Oh, my heart! I didn't know you were there.'

'I heard you squeal. What's that about?'

'Oh yeah, it's just I suppose I'm excited about my trip out west. You know, my rock study. The geography department has arranged accommodation for me and it looks amazing. Well, I mean the view from the window does!' Why did I lie? Why didn't I just say Henry McCormack arranged it? What was wrong with me? Why couldn't I be upfront with my husband?

'Good! I'm so glad you're excited about your trip!'

I smiled back, guiltily. He continued.

'In fact, I got you a little gift,' he said.

My face lit up and relief filled my heart. 'You did?' I reached out my hands expectantly, waiting for him to place his purchase from the red and white striped bag in them. The one I'd found in the recycling bin. But he didn't. He didn't reach for anything or hand me a dainty package.

'Oh no. It's online,' he said. 'I've emailed you a voucher.'

'A voucher?' I was a little disappointed.

'Yeah. For a facial. It's a skincare voucher.'

'Really?' This was surprising. *They don't package virtual vouchers in red and white striped gift bags, do they?*

'Yeah, you know, it's important to look after your skin, so I thought…'

'What? You mean, at my age? For us forty-year-olds?'

'God, no, Beatrice! I didn't mean it like that. I just thought it would give you a boost. Travelling can be quite draining and in turn, drying for the skin. It's an organ, you know, a living organ.'

'Yes, I know. What are you saying, Jeffrey?'

'Nothing, just enjoy the facial. I thought it would be a nice treat for you. You've got so much going on at the moment. Take an hour out for yourself, just for you, you know?'

'Oh, yeah, I suppose I do. The days are much longer now with the communications course two evenings a week.'

'Yeah, Beatrice, that's right. And that rock study. I mean, it's the most westerly point in Ireland, isn't it? Sure, that'll take you four or five hours to drive there. You'll be exhausted.'

'Yeah, I must Google to see how far it actually is. Just as well I've got the two nights booked. It would be too much driving for one night, wouldn't it?'

'Yeah, and I'm really glad you've got somewhere nice to stay. You never know, there might be a spa there!'

'What?'

'In the hotel! Maybe a luxurious spa, where you can go and pamper yourself!'

'Yeah, although I'll hardly need to do that if you've bought me a voucher for *Bella Mae Luxury Skincare*, will I?' I laughed.

He looked surprised. '*Bella Mae?* Oh no, it's not for that one. It's for a chemical peel in *Raise that Brow Now* in the city centre.'

He left me with my mouth hanging open and went into the bathroom to get ready for bed. *What the hell? A chemical peel?* What message was he sending me? And it wasn't for *Bella Mae*? So, what did he buy there? And, more importantly, who was it for?

I felt awful. This 'gift' or 'surprise' he got for me made me feel like I was ageing rapidly and he was dropping some major hints about it. I suppose Dr. Linda was ten years younger and looked it, with her tender, fresh face and blonder-than-mine hair. I went downstairs and sank into the couch. I picked up my laptop. I could hear Jeffrey's electric toothbrush buzzing upstairs. He was anal about his teeth. Dentists recommend two to three minutes of brushing, but he went on for at least five. I don't know how it didn't wake the children from their slumber.

I opened my emails and the latest one was from Jeffrey.

'This voucher entitles you to one light chemical peel. You will notice a visible improvement in your skin after one peel, but best results are obtained with multiple treatments over time.'

Oh great, this so-called 'gift' sounded like it was going to cost me a fortune in the long run. I read on.

'Chemical peels are intended to remove the outermost layers of the skin.'

And then I read the small print.

'To accomplish this task, the chosen peel solution induces a controlled injury to the skin.'

What, in the name of...? He calls this a gift? It's a curse. My husband had cursed me! An induced injury to the skin! The last time I was induced, a baby's head pushed itself through my uterus. A 'gift' from my husband should not remind me of this and should not invoke fear in me. Why would Jeffrey do this to me?

I went to bed and tried to be quiet. I didn't feel like engaging in conversation with him in case he expected me to thank him for my 'gift'. He turned towards me and reached out to touch my face.

'I've booked you in for Wednesday evening, Beatrice, for the chemical peel. They open late, until nine pm. That'll give you enough time to recover before your trip out west. You're going to love it, honey. I just know you will! Wait until you see your skin afterwards. You'll be amazed at how fresh and clear it looks!' With that, he kissed me on the cheek and rolled over. Within minutes, his breathing evened and I knew he'd fallen asleep.

As for me, I just lay there, eyes wide open, no doubt creating tension lines in my furrowed forehead. At least I'd have something with which to test the chemical peel.

No, I didn't sleep a wink.

Chapter Five

MY NEXT SLEEPLESS night arrived on the Thursday night before I was due to travel to Glan Mahogue. I was nervous. Nervous about the long journey, the amount of work involved in the project, but most of all, nervous about meeting Henry for the first time. We'd become quite familiar and comfortable with each other over the phone and I felt like it would be a special moment when we finally got to meet in the flesh. I knew from his enthusiastic voicemails and texts that he felt the same.

I awoke, exhausted, after plenty of anxious tossing and turning, but managed to pack my things and get ready to go by the time Jeffrey arrived home from the school run.

'Look at you, all bright eyed and bushy tailed! All ready to go?' He seemed genuinely excited for me. Just as excited as I was, in fact.

'Yes, I think I have everything. Oh, actually I forgot to pack my moisturiser. I'll just grab it.'

'No, Beatrice, don't worry about it. The SPF

isn't strong enough in that one anyway. I've packed the free samples you got from *Raise That Brow Now*. They're much better quality, SPF factor 50, and three sachets will be more than enough for the three days.'

'Oh, you did? You packed them for me?'

He laughed warmly. 'Yeah, sure I knew you'd forget.'

'Thanks, Jeffrey,' I wasn't going to waste time trying to figure this one out right now. But he seemed awfully concerned about my maturing skin. I was starting to feel paranoid about it. I always thought I had good skin, especially compared to my peers. I thought of my friend, Cara, with her furrowed brow. I think those creases in her forehead formed back in her twenties if I'm honest. But as for me, I'd inherited my mother's porcelain skin and never worried about premature ageing. Until now.

However, to give him his due, he was right about the chemical peel. It did give me the boost he said it would. And I enjoyed my pampering at the salon. The procedure itself was light and non-invasive. Fair play to him, he'd booked a gentle peel for me, so I didn't suffer any pain. It felt good and I looked radiant afterwards, which had a knock on effect of making me feel great. Jeffrey was delighted with the results.

And so was I. I had to admit, my skin looked

and felt abundantly clear.

✧ ✧ ✧

AFTER AN HOUR of motorway driving, I stopped to fill up the tank and grab a latte. I was beaming ear to ear. I must have looked ridiculous, but I didn't care. I felt so free and excited to be on a road trip on my own. This had never happened before. Not that I could recall, anyway. There were always three little hungry, noisy children in the back seats requiring us to stop every half hour to feed them or change nappies. No, this was different. I was my own boss and I had an endgame.

I played some 80s rock to pass the time in the car. I played it not only because I loved rock music, but also because I loved rock. Sedimentary, igneous, metamorphic—I loved all three. Rocks were better than humans, in my opinion. They were solid and dependable, large, hard and mountable, rough, smooth and everything in between. I shifted around in my bucket seat, getting aroused just thinking about rock. I turned up the music, full blast. 'We Will Rock You' by Queen blared and I thrust my pelvis to the beat. The image of Henry popped up in my mind, mid thrust. I couldn't wait to see this man. I checked the clock. Only another two hours to go, according to Google Maps.

✧ ✧ ✧

AS I DROVE through Roscommon, having reached 'The West', I thought of Jeffrey's well wishes. The gift, the moisturiser and the big smile on his face as I was leaving. He sure seemed happy to see me go. I knew he wouldn't look after the children all weekend. He'd need a break from them, a well-deserved break in fairness, and as ever, the grandparents were always ready to help out. He did everything for the kids. He got them dressed and out the door in the mornings, so I could hit the road early and beat the traffic. He made their school lunches, cooked nutritious meals for them and looked after my dietary requirements also. Whenever I offered to help, he insisted that he loved cooking and it was a pleasure to feed the family.

My parents loved him too. On many occasions, they referred to him as my 'perfect husband' and 'devoted father'. And they were right. He was all of those things, but they never found out he'd had an affair.

After having two pregnancies and three young children to show for it, I took a break from our marriage. I often went to sleep in the spare room and Jeffrey didn't like that. It was just that when I returned to work at the university, I was under so much pressure to update my curriculum and deliver lectures and tutorials, that I needed my eight hours of sleep. Mia had a habit of coming in for cuddles three or four times a night and I was so stressed, I couldn't get back to sleep. Jeffrey saw how tired I was and it was him who initially suggested I take the spare room. I guess he didn't expect I'd form a habit of sleeping there four nights a week.

The distance increased between us and the kids drained us of all our energy. I turned away from him first. I know I did. I remember the feeling of exhaustion. I craved sleep. I just wanted to put all my effort into looking after the children and any leftover scraps of energy were directed into preparing lectures. I knew I wasn't creating classes to the same standard as I had been pre-motherhood, but I did my best and got by. In the evenings, I withdrew from Jeffrey to work and craved both silence and alone time in bed. I worried that he might expect affection and I couldn't muster up any more than a fleeting peck on the lips before bed.

He felt neglected. He told me so and I did nothing about it, except devote more time to my lecturing career. I didn't mean to ignore his feelings of loneliness, but I think I saw it as a form of weakness. Like he was being needy or something. Why wasn't parenthood and work enough for him? Why was he pulling out of me when he could clearly see I had my hands full? I still loved him and I thought he'd just know that without me having to show him. Romantic gestures were not designed for mothers with three small children under two. He should have naturally known that. How did he even have space left inside him to desire his wife?

I guess that's when he strayed. I don't know how long his affair lasted or exactly when it started. All I knew was what he told me, when she ended it. She was the company doctor that he consulted when the twins were young and he put his back out. He subsequently met her at the office Christmas party. In his words, they 'hit it off and one thing led to another.' I hated his choice of phrasing. It was so clichéd, I thought. *Who says that in real life? It's just a line from the movies. Still, to this day, it makes me shudder when I think of it.*

Anyway, he confessed all, when she dumped him to marry her fiancé. He cried and pleaded with me to accept him back. He blamed the affair on a midlife crisis he was having and insisted it was nothing but a series of moments of madness. If she hadn't ended it when she did, he would have. And, I don't know, but at the time, I believed him. Maybe it was due to the guilt I felt when he opened up about how neglected he'd felt when the children came along and took over our lives. I knew I was culpable of shutting him out. I was tired, vulnerable and fragile, so I took it upon myself to accept my share of the blame for his affair.

He redeemed himself in the aftermath. We went for a short spell of couple's counselling and never referred to his infidelity after that. We just got on with the busyness of work and family life, while endeavouring to find some sort of balance in between. I think we managed well, even though he did the bulk of the household chores due to being able to work from home. It was only in recent weeks that I felt a mild sense of detachment. And then this morning, he looked so happy to see me go...

Oh gosh, I had to swerve to follow the signpost for Glan Mahogue. I didn't realise I was so close. I clocked the sign just in time. Only another 10km and I should hit the town, apparently. When I realised I was that close, I tried to take in my surroundings. The sky was moving in and out of greyness, so the landscape looked a dull shade of green. On the odd occasion when the sun peeped through, the greenery seemed to sparkle. And green it was!

I surveyed my panoramic view on the quiet country road I was travelling on. Nothing but grass and low stone walls were in sight, apart from the odd bungalow dotted throughout. They seemed like tiny dolls' houses in the distance, but, in reality, they were probably bigger than my four-bed detached house back in Dublin. It was just that they were so far away. I wondered what it would be like not to have immediate next door neighbours or shops nearby. I didn't think I'd survive for too long in the remote countryside. I liked living in a neighbourhood with local shops, schools and playgrounds for the kids. We were within walking distance of most of our requirements. That said, we hopped in the car more often than not. We just didn't have time for leisurely walks.

I pulled into the side of the road when I was just about a kilometre away from the one and only pub in the town, called *The Shed*, where I was meeting Henry. I brushed my mousey blonde, shoulder-length, straight hair and applied some blush pink lip gloss. I checked myself in the rearview mirror. I looked a little tired, but that was to be expected after a 4+ hour car journey. I rubbed hand cream on because I loved the smell of its lavender scent, but immediately wished I hadn't, because my hands were sweaty enough. The nerves were kicking in. I tidied up my side fringe and started the car. I drove slowly, trying to take in the scenery. I passed farmhouses and two signs advertising where to go for rods, tackle and bait. It clearly was a fishing village. I rolled down my window and smelled the sea. So salty and delightful. I wanted to observe more but was too distracted for that. I'd make time for sightseeing later.

The Shed appeared before me to my right. I didn't go to the carpark, but rather pulled in on the opposite side of the road. A figure caught my eye. A head of dark, curly hair, phone in hand, looking down, sitting on the wall outside. It was him. It was Henry. I knew it was. I got out of the car and began walking towards him. Hands sweaty, heart racing and knees shaking. I tried to slow down. He still had his head stuck in his phone, so he didn't see me approaching. My shaking knees got the better of me and I stumbled a little. He heard that and looked up. I stopped in my tracks, as he stood up to greet me.

'Oh', I said aloud. He was shorter than I imagined. I thought he'd be taller than that. He wasn't tall at all. He was relatively short. Not a short man, per se. Not exactly a shortass, but considerably shorter than I hoped. Then he opened his mouth to say something.

'Ah Beatrish, is it you? You're here at last!' He beamed ear to ear and I almost fell over.

'Henry! Where are your teeth?' My nerves quickly turned into disgust and horror. I felt bile rising from the pit of my stomach. This was not at all what I'd been expecting. He had no teeth!

'What? Oh, my teeth! Oh, messing around on the GAA pitch. My older brother knocked them out a few weeks ago.'

'I don't...I don't understand! What? So, you've had no teeth for a few weeks? All that time we were texting and talking and you had no teeth in your mouth?'

'Ah now, Beatrish, calm down. It's only the top front four that got knocked out. I have the rest, sure, look.' With that, he opened his mouth wide, very wide, too wide. And all I could see were no upper teeth. I felt faint. He continued.

'Sure, the dentist has them ready for me these past few days. I just haven't had time to collect them yet, what with preparing for your visit.'

'Henry, what could be more important than collecting your teeth?'

'You! You, arriving in my hometown of Glan Mahogue, of course!' He smiled toothlessly. I sat down. I had to. I put my hand to my head. I guess that might be a contributing factor as to why he couldn't seem to pronounce my name correctly.

'Beatrish, if it means that much to you, I'll take a spin up to the dentist now and get them. He's a friend of mine. We all know each other in Glan Mahogue. Would that make you feel more comfortable if I got my teeth fitted today? Like, this afternoon?'

'Yes, yes, I think it would.' I despaired at this stage. I felt like such a fool. And to think I'd built myself up for this and allowed myself to feel excited. I whimpered into my hands.

'Beatrish, would you like a drink? I'll go in and get you one and bring it out. You must be parched after the long journey. What'll you have?'

'Sauvignon blanc.'

'Hmm? What did you say?'

'White wine.'

'Oh, right, I'll see if they have it. I'm more of a Smithwicks man myself.' He sauntered off into the pub. I contemplated doing a runner. I could disappear now and not come back. I'd never have to see this toothless clown again and... But then I thought of the actual reason why I was here. The rock study. As the saying goes, I was caught between a rock and a hard place, but I couldn't let the geography department down. After all, they gave me Friday and Monday off as travel days. I turned around when I heard footsteps. Oh heavens, a full bottle. He got me a full bottle of wine!

'Henry! I meant a glass! A glass of wine!'

'Beatrish, you can have a glass and take it with you for later, back at the...'

'But my car, Henry. I have to drive. If I have more than a glass I won't be able to...'

'Hahahaha!' he guffawed and flashed his gums at me again. 'You won't get stopped for drunk driving here, Beatrish! It's not like in Dublin. Like I said, we all know each other and...'

'Right, right, pour me a glass, so.' I knocked it

back. He raised his brow questioningly. 'Yes', I answered and held out my glass for another. I decided I missed Jeffrey, just then, at that very moment. He always knew when I needed a refill. He never looked puzzled like Henry. He always knew. He just knew.

My eyes watered.

Chapter Six

'EH, BEATRISH', HENRY whispered after a few minutes. He seemed to realise I was 'having a moment'. I looked up, glassy eyed. 'Eh, it's just I'm gonna get myself to the dentist now for the teeth fitting. He said to come before four o'clock. I'll be the guts of an hour. Will you be okay here?' He delicately left the bottle of wine on the ground by my feet.

'You're leaving me here? On the wall, outside the pub? With nothing but a bottle of wine? For an hour? Here, in the middle of nowhere?'

'Yeah, yeah, is that okay with you? You can, eh, use the facilities inside in *The Shed*, if you need to, em, y'know.'

'Oh, yeah.' I looked back towards *The Shed*. It matched its name. It was completely unpretentious, unlike the pubs in Dublin city centre. It really did seem to be a shed in which someone obtained a licence to operate as a local drinking establishment.

'What's that building? There' I pointed—

'beside *The Shed*?'

'Oh, that's *The Bed*.'

'The what?'

'*The Bed*, our local nightclub. Fairly decent after hours licence. You could stay there all night if you wanted to. That's why they called it *The Bed*.'

I swallowed, just trying to take it all in. 'So, it's *The Bed* beside *The Shed*?'

He smiled, a close-mouthed one, I noted with relief. A little smile escaped my lips too. *The Shed* and *The Bed*. Jeez, where the heck did the geography department in UCND think they were sending me? I couldn't help but laugh.

'Are you okay, Beatrish? It's just a minute ago you were crying and now you're laughing. It's not exactly clear to me what's going on. Is it the wine? Gone to your head already, is it?'

'Hmm, yeah, maybe that's it, Henry. It must be the wine.' I picked up the bottle by my feet and refilled my glass. Right to the top this time. He nodded and walked off towards his car. As he drove by me, en route to the dentist, he rolled down his window and hollered.

'Welcome to Glan Mahogue, Beatrish!'

✧ ✧ ✧

IT WASN'T LONG before I needed the facilities, so I headed into *The Shed*. It was rustic, to say the least. I could tell it was the local, popular hotspot from the graffitied walls in the cubicle and the subtle, stubborn scent of urine, both in the toilets and the corridor leading to them. Anyway, I managed. I was quite glad the mirrors were so foggy, because I didn't want to see a clear reflection of myself at this point. Not the way I was feeling. I washed my hands with cold water, dirtied them trying to extract the soap from the greasy, empty dispenser and rinsed them again. Unsurprisingly, I discovered the hand dryer didn't work, so I shook them in the hopes they would air dry.

I checked my watch. Only a half hour had passed since Henry left for the dentist. I missed home already. I went outside and sat back down on the wall. I took out my phone and rang Jeffrey.

'Hey there! How was your journey?' Jeffrey sounded sprightly.

'Oh, yeah, well, I made it here anyway,' I replied.

'You okay, Beatrice?'

'Yeah, yeah, I'm fine. It was just a long journey and I suppose...' I yawned before continuing, 'I'm tired.'

'Well, what's it like there? How is Glen Minogue?' he asked, with a bit too much enthusiasm.

'It's Glan Mahogue, Jeffrey! It's, it's...well, I haven't really seen much of it yet.'

'Oh yeah, sure I suppose you're not long there. So, tell me, what's the hotel like? Send me a photo of the view, will you?'

'Em, well, I kind of haven't made it there yet. I'm, em, I'm waiting for my guide to return.'

'Oh, so where are you now?'

'I'm having refreshments while I wait for him. Hehhh! Oh, and I think I've got the, hehhhh, hiccups.'

'Are you drinking, Beatrice? Are you okay?'

'Hehhh! Yes, just light refreshments is all. Hehhh! I'm fine, Jeffrey,' I reassured him as I drained the bottle of Sauvignon Blanc into my glass.

'Okay, Bea, if you say so. And where did you say your guide was?'

'Hehhh! He's at the dentist.'

'The dentist? At this time? On a Friday evening?'

'Yeah, it was kind of an emergency, I suppose.'

'Are you waiting there all alone in the middle of nowhere?'

'Hehhh! Yes.'

'Beatrice, that's awful! Especially after the long journey you've had. You should contact the admin at uni. They must be able to do something for you. Maybe arrange another guide or...'

I spotted Henry's car approaching. 'No, Jeffrey, it's okay. He's back. I should get to my hotel soon.

Give the kids a kiss from me, okay?'

'Yeah, they're so excited about the sleepover in Granny's tonight. I'm just leaving, actually. Eager to get home at this stage.'

'What? Oh, you're not staying with them? I thought you were all staying over?'

'Ah Beatrice, why would I do that? And miss out on a free gaff? Are you mad?'

'Hehhh! Oh, right, yes, sounds lovely.' And what will you be getting up to, I wondered. Ordering more invisible gifts from *Bella Mae Luxury Skincare*? Stocking up on some anti-aging creams for your good wife? Hmmm... 'Look, I have to go now. I'll text you later, okay?'

'Good luck, honey! I hope the hiccups clear soon!'

'Hehhh! So do I. Bye Jeffrey.' I knew I'd have to ask him outright about that red and white stripey bag in the recycling bin. I hated the thoughts of entering into an awkward conversation like that, but I'd be driven demented if I didn't get to the bottom of it soon.

Henry walked towards me and flashed a pearly white smile.

'Oh, wow, Henry! Hehhh! Amazing! They look great!' I was genuinely impressed. It made such a difference.

'Yeah, I'm delighted with them. Way more respectable than my original teeth too! I'll be thanking my bro for knocking them out, I will! Hahahahah!' He opened his mouth wide to laugh and I examined his teeth again. Truly spectacular dentistry. I made a mental note to look up Glan Mahogue's local dental practice. I knew I needed a checkup soon.

Henry picked up my wine bottle and looked very impressed with how I'd emptied it. I noticed a little dimple on his right cheek as he smiled. Ah, it was very cute. I found I was more able to look at his face now that he had teeth in his gums. It was more conducive for me to examine him with his dentures firmly in place. He told me he'd be back in a minute and I assumed he needed to use the facilities, but he arrived back with another bottle of white wine. I was aghast.

'Hehhh! Henry, what's that for?'

'You seemed to like it, Beatrice! C'mon, we'll take it with us. I'll drive. You can leave your car here. Just go and grab your overnight bag. The roads around here would confuse you.'

'Another bottle of wine? Really? I haven't, hehhh, eaten yet. I feel like I'll collapse if I don't get food soon.'

'C'mon then. You won't get a meal in *The Shed*. Let's go.'

He held out his hand for me to take it and follow him. I looked around. I had nowhere else to go and I couldn't drive, not in my state, that was for sure. Hopefully, the rock study could wait until tomorrow morning. I needed to go and sleep this one off. I took his hand, got my bag as instructed, and allowed him lead me to his car.

✧ ✧ ✧

'WE'LL TAKE THE coast road, Beatrice. It's a bit longer, but it'll be worth it. You'll see.'

'Okay. Actually, I've got my camera in my bag, so I'll tell you if I want to stop and...' Then, I got distracted because I saw the sea. I rolled down the window and inhaled the salt in the air.

'Can we go there now, Henry? I'd like to go to the beach. Now?'

'Yeah, we'll stop off. It might sober you up, hehehe! And then we'll get some food. We're getting close now.'

We didn't talk again. I sat back and admired the view. I actually felt like I was in a different country altogether, so different was it to the east coast—much wilder and windier. As soon as he pulled over, I jumped out of the car and felt the cobwebs getting blown out of my head. I looked at him and laughed. 'Yep, it did the trick!' The sea air drained my brain of alcoholic toxins and blew the hiccups away.

I ran along the stony beach and dodged the ebb and flow of the incoming waves on the shoreline. I felt free. I felt sober. In fact, my mind felt abundantly clear and fresh. I laughed to myself. If I drank a whole bottle of wine by myself in Dublin, it would take me days to recover. But here, the air was so restorative and unpolluted, it cured me immediately. Then I tripped over a rather large rock and Henry ran to my aid.

'Let's get some food into you, Beatrice. You're still hammered.'

'Am I? I feel fine', I pleaded, but saw my palms were scratched and bleeding. 'Yeah, okay, sure we'll come back here tomorrow, won't we?'

We got back in the car and after a few minutes Henry started making a drum roll sound. He stopped the car.

'Well, Beatrice, what do you think?'

'Huh?' I looked around. 'Am I dreaming?' I asked. All I could see was, well, nothing. No hotel in sight, although one little structure caught my eye. A caravan. Parked on a low-lying cliff edge. Overlooking the beach. The beach—I looked again. It was familiar to me. I'd seen this beach before. Oh, it was the 'view' from my window that Henry sent me.

'But, but, where is my hotel, Henry?'

'Welcome to the most westerly point in Ireland, Beatrice! Your home for the weekend!' he beamed.

'Excuse me?'

'Oh sorry, I mean OUR home for the weekend!

I wouldn't have you staying in that thing on your own, in case the winds increased overnight. Can't be too careful. The bloody weather is so unpredictable, especially around here.'

I didn't get out of the car when he did. I couldn't. I couldn't move. I was paralysed. How on earth could I be so naive as to let a total stranger book my accommodation for the weekend? What was wrong with me? The admin at uni offered to arrange it, but I got sucked in by Henry and blindly trusted his judgement. I couldn't even vent with anyone now, as I'd kept my textual relationship with him a secret.

I sank back in my bucket seat and decided this must be a midlife crisis I was going through—when you regress in your forties and turn into a stupid, naive, vulnerable teenager taking risks. I guess this is what Jeffrey went through when he leapt into bed with Linda. Tears filled my eyes all of a sudden. I guess I'd never really dealt with the emotional toll of his affair. Our couple's counselling was all about moving forward in a practical way. We were encouraged not to dwell on events of the past. That approach may have suited Jeffrey, but it didn't suit me. I had hurt locked inside me. I could feel it now. The sea air drew salty tears from me and they streamed down my face. I just sat there in the car, crying and making a yelping sound, a bit like a cat when someone steps on its paw. I couldn't stop. What had my life turned into? A defective marriage, a failing career and now, a disastrous attempt at an extramarital flirtation.

Chapter Seven

I LOOKED AT Henry walking to the cliff edge to admire the beach. To be fair, he was giving me my moment again. He seemed to be a sensitive sort. He must have heard the relentless squealing from the car. I was sure the wind carried it to his ears. I couldn't believe I'd built him up into a fantasy, though. He was disappointingly shorter than I imagined, lacking his four front teeth while having the audacity to bare his gums, and now I find out he lives in a caravan! An old, rusty one at that, from what I could see. The green and white colour of it reminded me of the Irish dancing caravan in *Father Ted*. It was about the same size too. I despaired and hung my head. Henry gave me a fright when he asked if I was getting out of the car.

'Em, not right now.'

He pointed. 'This is the view I sent you.'

'Mmhmm, yeah, I'll take a look in a minute.'

'Will I bring out a glass, Beatrice? Would that help? The last time you were crying, the glass of wine seemed to help.'

I looked down at the bottle by my feet. He was right. It did help. Wine always helped. I picked it up. Screw top—amazing! I opened it and took a few swigs. Still cold. *The Shed* had topnotch refrigeration. I'd give it that.

'Oh, right, so, you probably don't need a glass. I'll go get you something to eat. That might help.'

He left me guzzling from the bottle and went into the caravan. I sat there with my bottle of sauvignon blanc in hand, wondering if this was what rock-bottom felt like. I thought back to the early days of my relationship with Jeffrey, when I was madly in love and on the cusp of achieving my professional dreams to become a geography lecturer. *And look at me now*. Look what those deluded dreams turned into—me, pretending to be a professional researcher for a university project, when in reality, I was sitting in a stranger's car swigging from a cheap wine bottle having done nothing for my assignment. My husband was most likely embarking on a second affair with God knows who and I was in the firing line at the university for my crap lecture delivery.

My shoulders jumped in shock at my dire situation and I cried again. I knew in my heart I wouldn't forgive Jeffrey for a second affair. I didn't have it in me to forgive him twice. Once was enough. He better be prepared for a separation if he was engaging in another indiscretion, because I wouldn't stand for it again. I'd best get my shit together ASAP and take this rock study seriously, along with the communications course, if I wanted to hold onto my job. It was time for me to plan for single motherhood and become more independent. I just couldn't get that red and white striped bag out of my mind. Who was the lucky recipient? Who was it? God knows, it wasn't me.

All this catastrophizing about rock-bottom got me thinking about rocks. I decided I'd like to have an actual rock under my bottom, so I got out of the car to find one.

✧ ✧ ✧

HENRY FOUND ME on my chosen slab, hugging my bottle of wine. He handed me a plate of fried fish and a fork.

'Here, I caught this early this morning. It's plaice.'

I looked down. It looked like it was cooked to perfection in a little butter and oil. I noticed he'd seasoned it well and served it with a little salad on the side.

'Thank you, Henry. This looks delicious.' With that, I tore into it and gobbled it up. I was ravenous. He brought out more and I devoured that too. He was delighted I liked it so much. I didn't mention that I was so hungry, I would have eaten shells from the beach at this stage. He didn't need to know that. He thoughtfully, brought out a pint of water too. I admired his intuition. He seemed to just know I needed that, pretty desperately too.

Henry sat down on the grass beside me and waited for me to finish. He was very patient. I didn't feel the need to rush.

'Aren't you eating?' I asked him.

'Well, that was my portion, but I'm delighted you liked it so much. I'll get something later.'

'Oh God, you must think I'm a pig. Sorry!'

He laughed and I caught a glimpse of his pearly whites again. I was searching for them now. So impressive. And it changed his whole face. He looked way more like the fisherman in the photo he'd sent. THE photo. The one I went to bed with on numerous occasions. He interrupted my thoughts.

'Beatrice, I'm not trying to pry or anything and I know we only met each other in person a few hours ago, but you seem quite emotional. Is there anything the matter?'

I took a deep breath and then let out a little chuckle. It's just that he asked so innocently why I seemed like a raving lunatic. He phrased it so delicately. He was kind. I looked at him and smiled. I was glad that even though I'd established he probably wasn't the man of my dreams, at least he was a decent sort and maybe we could be friends.

'Henry, my husband, Jeffrey, had an affair.'

'Ah, the bastard. Dump him!'

'Well, no, it's not that simple. We have a family, three young kids. The twins, Mia and Lauren, are five and Daniel is three. We're a team. We work really well as a family. I wouldn't be able to pursue my geography career without Jeffrey's support. I need him. And...he's such a good father and...husband, even. He looks after all of us so well, and he loves us and we love him.'

'But he had an affair, Beatrice. You can't trust him.'

I sighed. A deep, heavy one. Then I poured some wine into my empty pint glass and handed Henry the bottle. 'Here, have a swig.'

'Ah no, it's yours. Hang on, I'll be back. He took my plate and went into the caravan. He came back with a can of Smithwicks.

'Cheers!' he beamed.

We drank and talked. Henry had never been married, but he was hoping to meet someone one day. In his words, he'd 'exhausted all the local talent', so he tended to get fiercely excited when visitors, such as myself, arrived in Glan Mahogue.

'But, Henry, you knew I was married, didn't you?'

He fobbed me off. 'Ah, regular rules of society

aren't heeded much this far west.' I had to laugh in response. What kind of a town was this? It started to get cold, so we decided to go for a walk on the beach.

'No running this time, Beatrice!' Henry warned. 'I don't want any more injuries on my turf, okay?'

I promised I wouldn't take off like a crazy woman. He'd seen enough madness from me in the last few hours. Besides, it was getting dark and I was starting to feel tired. We stood and watched the sun set. I wished I'd remembered to bring along my camera, but Henry assured me I'd see it again. He didn't want me racing back to the car and missing it. I was glad. The blue got dark, turning to a navy-grey and the orange sun glistened, sending a delicate golden light beneath the clouds, until eventually they covered it. It was so special. I felt privileged to witness it. I turned to Henry.

'Thank you. That image will remain with me forever.'

'Ah, that's the wine talking. You'll forget this tomorrow, but don't worry, we'll see it again. I see it almost every evening from my caravan and I never tire of it.'

We walked back towards his humble abode. I needed to go to the toilet, so he let me in. The bathroom wasn't hard to find in his pokey little establishment. I was shocked that he lived here and even more astounded that he thought I'd prefer to stay here than in a swanky hotel. Bless him, though, there was something endearingly naive about him all the same. I had a quick look around and wondered where I was supposed to sleep, given there was only one single bedroom. He hardly thought we'd both fit in there, did he? Oooh, that was a bit creepy if that was the case. I suddenly felt quite vulnerable. I met him outside.

'Well, Beatrice, what do you think of my caravan?'

'Yeah, it's, em, lovely, but small.'

'I tidied it up for you and gave it a lick of paint. Hope you can't still smell the fresh paint, can you?'

'No, no, I could just smell fish. I was wondering, em, well, where you were planning to sleep if you were offering me your caravan?'

'Oh, good question and you're right to ask. You Dublin girls don't beat about the bush! You can take the bedroom and the little dining table converts into a single bed. I've a sleeping bag for myself. I've done it before and I'll be grand out there with the scent of fried fish still on the pan.'

'Oh, I see. Look, Henry, as I told you, I'm married and I just don't think it would be right for me to spend the night in your caravan. It's a bit, em, I don't know, intimate, considering we hardly know each other.'

'Beatrice, I'll pitch my tent on the grass out

here if it would make you feel more comfortable?'

'Ah God, no, Henry, I wouldn't ask you to do that. Look, I'll sleep in my car. Can you collect it for me and bring it here?' He nodded in response.

'The seat reclines fully and maybe I'll just get a blanket from you. I'll be fine, honestly.' He looked a bit heartbroken. He'd gone to a lot of trouble for me, what with painting and tidying the caravan and getting his front teeth fitted at such short notice. All for me. That said, there was no way I was sleeping in his caravan tonight. I'd drive back to Dublin, if I wasn't so pissed, but I'd consumed almost two full bottles of wine, so I definitely wasn't going anywhere tonight.

I gave him my keys and he brought back my car, leaving his own in the carpark of *The Shed*. He gave me a nice heavy, woollen blanket that smelled of fish and told me he'd leave the caravan unlocked in case I needed the facilities during the night. 'In fact', he said, 'I never lock it,' which didn't surprise me in the slightest. I switched on the lights in the car, as it was pitch black and the wind was howling. I turned on the engine to heat up, locked the doors and snuggled under the briny blanket. When I was warm enough, I turned off the engine, double checked that I was securely locked in and somehow, quite miraculously, fell asleep.

✧ ✧ ✧

THE RISING SUN woke me from my slumber. At first, I didn't know where I was, but the fishy aroma from the blanket reminded me. I checked my watch. Barely five am. 'Uhhh.' I squirmed. The ungodly hour and my sore head made me want to cry. I reached for the glove compartment. Thank God, my emergency stash of painkillers was in there. I knocked them back with the dregs of my bottle of water, left over from the car journey yesterday. I lay back and tried to rest, but I couldn't settle. I started to get a little panicky. What the hell was I doing? This trip was not going as planned. I was a professional. A lecturer. I mean, if my students could see me now. I was supposed to present the findings of my rock study to them and so far, all I had to show for my trip out west was two empty bottles of sauvignon blanc. Right, that's it, I decided, I'm going home. I'd tell the geography department that I had to reschedule my trip due to illness. Anyway I was too hungover and fragile to get any decent work done today.

I got out of the car, folded the blanket and left it outside Henry's caravan, hoping the fresh air might get rid of the fishy smell. It badly needed to be aired. I took one last look at the wild Atlantic Ocean and promised I'd be back. The ocean and the rocks would understand. I had to sort my head out. And my marriage. And my career. The ocean and the rocks would wait for me. I'd ring Henry later to explain. I didn't want to disturb him now and he might try to talk me out of leaving. I hit the road and drove to the nearest 24-hour petrol station to use the facilities. Of course, it was 50 miles away and I nearly peed my pants, but I made it and got a supersized latte and a sausage roll. I sat in the car and devoured them, thankful that they were giving me some much needed sustenance for the journey ahead.

Chapter Eight

THE COFFEE HELPED set my mind straight. I was on a mission now. Going home to talk things through with Jeffrey. The kids would still be at their sleepover, so we could sit down and properly chat without any disturbances. I might even try out some of my newly learned communicative techniques, like active listening and responsive questioning. It was so obvious to me now that myself and Jeffrey didn't communicate properly. We went through the motions of our busy lives, tending to the children, involving the grandparents, running a bustling household, maintaining two demanding careers and just making sure everyone was fed, clothed, warm and happy. But we didn't have time for each other anymore.

It was only now with the distance between us that I realised how our relationship was suffering. The intimacy was gone. Gone since the twins were born if I'm honest, but we never got it back. Then, when Jeffrey strayed, that was a second blow to our marriage. My eyes watered at the wheel when I thought about this. I know I eventually forgave him and accepted him back, but we never put the effort into our relationship after that. We never fought to get back what we once had. We just returned to our everyday lives and neither of us rocked the boat since then.

Granted, the grandparents were always ready and willing to babysit, but we only took advantage when there was something on, like a wedding or an office party that the kids weren't invited to. We rarely went out together on a date. I suppose because Jeffrey was such an amazing cook, it was easier to put the kids to bed early and have a nice, quiet meal at the kitchen table with a bottle of wine. Why we didn't communicate then baffled me. We usually ended up talking about work. I guess we both had such interesting careers that there was always something new to share. Jeffrey, with an exciting IT project to get his teeth into and, as he was a freelance contractor, there was great diversity between projects. Of course, I always had geography news or my latest research to impart with him and we kept the conversation going with that.

Not to mention the kids, grandparents, friends, or even just the shopping list for the week ahead. We generally seemed to avoid discussing ourselves, our feelings and our marriage. Was it me? Was I at fault? I clearly had poor communication skills.

That much had been proven of late. Did I simply not want to confront our failing relationship to avoid the hassle of trying to work things out?

Had Jeffrey made an effort? Maybe all the romantic meals he cooked and bottles of wine after the kids went to bed were supposed to encourage us to share. Maybe he had been making an effort all along and I'd overlooked it to avoid reliving the nightmare of his infidelity.

Just knowing that I wasn't enough for him was still eating me up inside. Even when the twins were young and I craved nothing but sleep, he was still enough for me. I never wanted anyone else. I knew it was a phase our marriage was going through, but felt confident we would get our chemistry back as soon as we got our sleep back. I just put our intimacy on hold. *I had you on hold, Jeffrey. And then you went and ruined everything with HER! Damn it!*

Oh, I found myself bursting into tears at the wheel. I slowed down, as my eyes clouded over. It was abundantly clear I still had many issues to deal with on the back of Jeffrey's affair. I needed to get home. We urgently required a much overdue heart-to-heart.

✧ ✧ ✧

I WIPED MY eyes and caught a glimpse of myself in

the rearview mirror. Christ, I looked awful. My eyes were still puffy and red from crying, my hair was windswept and scraggly from the beach and my skin looked dry and salty. As I approached our house on Beechfield Close, I pulled into the vacant dwelling opposite ours to freshen up. It was up for sale, but there would be no viewings this early on a Saturday morning. Usually, they held open viewings from two to four pm in the afternoons. I rummaged through my handbag and found my hairbrush. I attempted to detangle, but it was tied in knots from the sea air. I supposed I could leg it straight to the bathroom, but I didn't want Jeffrey seeing me like this. I'd tidy myself up a little before...

But what was that? A sudden movement caught my eye. I caught it in the rearview mirror, just by chance, as I was brushing over my side fringe. Was it Mrs. Johnson next door going out for her daily stroll? I peered in the mirror. No, it wasn't Mrs. Johnson's front door. It was ours.

Was Jeffrey already leaving to collect the kids? Maybe he had brunch plans with Granny and Grandad. Maybe he'd seen me pull in and was coming out to greet me, to find out why I'd cut short my field trip. My eyes widened when I discovered the person exiting our front door was clearly not Jeffrey. I gulped when I saw a tall, young, slim woman exiting. Hang on a sec, who the hell was that? Did Jeffrey get a new cleaner behind my back or something? I didn't move, but kept looking. I didn't want her to notice me.

I slowly, very mindfully released my gulp in efforts to restart the breathing process. I choked on my next breath. This was difficult and I found I could barely inhale. I lowered my hand to rest it on my tummy, but the hairbrush got stuck in my fringe. I narrowed my eyes to get a closer look.

The woman on the doorstep looked pristine and young and very, very happy. Jeffrey was behind her, still chatting animatedly. He looked very, very happy too. What was going on? She was far too glamorous to be a cleaner. *Silly me.* She had skinny jeans, strappy wedges and a blazer that fitted her perfectly. She looked dressed up. Her hair was in an immaculate short, straight bob and her face was made up to the nines. Even from across the road, I could see her defined eyebrows and red lipstick. She was striking, like a model, and laughing with my husband.

I didn't want to move in case the hairbrush that was accidentally stuck in my fringe would swing and draw attention to me. I tried taking deep breaths, while one question ran through my mind like burning lava, scorching my throbbing brain. WHY WAS A TALL, GLAMOROUS, YOUNG, SLIM WOMAN IN SKINNY JEANS, HIGH WEDGES AND A TIGHT-FITTING BLAZER

WITH A CUTE BOB AND FACE FULL OF MAKEUP LAUGHING WITH MY HUSBAND, WHILE SAYING GOODBYE TO HIM ON OUR DOORSTEP ON A SATURDAY MORNING WHEN HE HAD THE HOUSE TO HIMSELF?

I remained still and calm, but repeated the question in my head several times, until she finally turned to walk away. I could see her face, closer now. She was still smiling and looking divine. The closer she came, the clearer she became and I realised she couldn't have been more than twenty-one. Oh, Lord heavens above. He was having another, more severe midlife crisis. And to think I was jealous of Linda because she was ten years younger. This doll looked about twenty years younger than both of us!

How could he? How could he do this to me? Again? And to our family? The kids? Our parents? And what was he thinking bringing her back to our house? Our family home? I mean, did they have sex in our bed? I covered my mouth to stop myself screaming. Jeffrey had closed the front door and his latest fling was strutting herself down to the bus stop, it seemed. I struggled to turn my head as the hairbrush dangled from my fringe and just about caught a glimpse of her on the corner, seemingly waiting for the bus.

And what was this? I couldn't believe my eyes! She lit up a cigarette! A smoker? Jeffrey—with a smoker? He hated smoking. I had to give up my social smoking because of him. He said it was a deal breaker. And here he was shagging a twenty-year-old chain smoker! This didn't make sense! How could he? I thought about our bedsheets. Would I smell stale cigarette smoke from them? Was he planning to wash them before I was due to arrive home? This didn't bear thinking about. I was so enraged. I didn't know what to do. I yanked the hairbrush from my fringe and whimpered at the pain of it. Then I pulled out of the driveway and just started driving. Away from Beechfield Close. Away from our family home. Away from Jeffrey.

I blasted *Appetite for Destruction* by Guns N' Roses and headbanged to the beat of 'Nightrain'. How could he? How could he do this to me? To us? And a smoker? What a bloody hypocrite! I'd never listen to him again about health and wellbeing matters or accept any more skincare advice from him. In bed with a smoker! In our bed with a smoker! Young enough to be his daughter! I couldn't...I couldn't go on. This was hurting me too much. I felt my head and it was throbbing. I spotted a sign for a petrol station ahead and pulled in as soon as I could.

Oh wow, I didn't realise I'd crossed the county border and was already in Co Kildare. I seemed to be on the same road I'd travelled on earlier. I guess it was familiar to me and I'd just let the car take me, without properly thinking about where I was going. I went into the station shop to buy water and cigarettes, internally giving Jeffrey the middle finger as I forked out €14 for a pack of twenty.

I returned to the car and knocked back two more painkillers with the water. Oh, how I needed pain relief right now. Then I cursed myself that I'd forgotten to buy a lighter for the smokes and my fancy car didn't seem to have one inbuilt, or else I just couldn't find it. I drove on, thinking about how much I wanted to smoke right now. How much I wanted to do anything and everything to spite Jeffrey. To make him angry. How could he do this to me?

I drove on. And on. I drove through Co Kildare and into Meath and Westmeath. It was therapeutic to concentrate on the driving. I had to focus on something or I would have gone mad. I realised when I hit Roscommon where I was actually headed. I was going back to Glan Mahogue. Back to Henry. Sure, I had nowhere else to go!

I MUST HAVE driven fairly fast, for it was only shortly after 3pm when I pulled up beside Henry's caravan. I got out and took in the spectacular view. I inhaled the salty, sea air and felt a sense of calm befalling me. The ocean and the rocks would help cure me, I reassured myself. I spotted movement on the beach and saw a boat coming to shore. Could it be Henry? I made my way down on the jagged rocks and slid a little on the grassy bits and small stones. Yes, as I got closer, I realised it was Henry. I was glad to see him. In fact, it warmed my heart to see him getting out of his fishing boat.

He spotted me too and waved. I could see his big smile and black curly hair blowing in the wind. As I got closer, I realised he wasn't actually that short. Maybe I was a bit harsh on him yesterday. I'd say he was about as tall as me, which was slightly short for a man, but at least he wasn't smaller than me. We were about the same height, I'd say.

'Beatrice, what did you get up to? Did you go and see the local sights?' He sounded jovial and the lilt in his west of Ireland accent inspired warmth in me.

'Henry, you won't believe where I've been!'

'It's okay, Beatrice. I think I know.'

'Oh, you do? How?' I wasn't expecting that.

'*The Shed* opens for a liquid lunch. All the tourists go there on a Saturday afternoon and I know how much you love the wine.'

Oh no, he thinks I'm an alcoholic. Of course he does! Why wouldn't he? I've given him no reason to think otherwise.

'Em, well, no, Henry. I haven't had a drink today at all.'

'Ah, that's your own business, Beatrice. Here, look what I caught! It'll make a tasty supper for us later!' He showed me some fish. I didn't know exactly what type it was, but it was dead fish and I thanked him very much.

We walked back to his caravan and discussed the seaweed varieties we passed along the way, namely dillisk and some carrageen moss. I waited for him outside his caravan, as he put the fish away and I smiled to myself. I never discussed important stuff like seaweed with Jeffrey. NEVER! And then, I smelled the fish from Henry's caravan and realised I much preferred the scent of fish to the stench of cigarette smoke. MUCH PREFERRED IT!

When Henry reappeared, I asked him for a light. I sat on a rock and smoked for the first time in ten years. Screw you, Jeffrey Walsh, I thought to myself.

'Em, Beatrice, it's nearly four o'clock and we haven't, well, we haven't done much work yet for your project. When you're finished smoking, do you think we should start, or are you planning to have a drink with that?'

'Oh Lord, Henry, you're right! The project! We'd better get started.' I outed the cigarette on the rock. 'I'll go get my folder from the car. We'll start crossing some stuff off the list.' Brilliant! He was a genius! This was exactly what I needed right now to get my mind off the events of this morning. I needed to get stuck into this rock study. We had loads to get through. I can do this, I told myself. Not as much time as I'd like to get it all done, but I was ready to start. Now that the painkillers had kicked in, I was good to go.

Chapter Nine

WE STAYED ON task for the next few hours and I lashed through my to-do list. I could see why Henry was chosen to assist me in this project. There was nothing he didn't know about the locality and if there was a question he couldn't answer, he knew the right person to ask. Everyone was so generous with their time and I found myself falling for the soft accents and friendly, relaxed characters.

It was nearly eight o'clock by the time we made it back to his caravan. I desperately needed a shower, so Henry prepared our supper while I freshened up. I got changed in his bedroom and admired the paintings of the local landscape he'd hung on the walls. Everything about him and belonging to him was making me smile.

He produced a chilled bottle of sauvignon blanc from his tiny fridge and the fish and chips were salty, yummy, fresh and delicious. Again, I was smiling, and everytime I looked at Henry, he smiled back. I noticed there really was a touch of the ocean in his eyes. Not just the colour, but there was a wildness in them too.

He was so unlike Jeffrey. Henry was rugged, easy going, earthy, a grafter and a 'take me as I am' kind of guy, while Jeffrey wore a suit even when he worked from home. Jeffrey was anal about his appearance, a symptom of the affliction he'd acquired of being strikingly good looking. I used to be jealous of him when we were dating and even more jealous of all the attention he got. Heads turned for Jeffrey and yes, he knew it. He got his sallow skin, luscious black hair and deep brown eyes from his mother. She was a beauty queen in her day, apparently. Good looks ran in his family. But when I looked at Henry this evening, I could appreciate an alternative kind of good looking. So different from my husband, so abundantly different, in fact, that one could say they were polar opposites. I sat back and lit another cigarette, sated after the meal, while Henry opened a second bottle of wine.

✧ ✧ ✧

IT CAME OUT. I couldn't help it. I told Henry all about my catastrophic morning and he said everything I wanted him to say in return. He cursed Jeffrey to no end and called him every name under the sun, but my favourite was 'that double-crossing shleeveen'.

'Yes, yes, he is. Exactly that indeed! What you just said!' I agreed whole-heartedly and took another gulp of my wine. He folded up the dining table to make us more comfortable. The seats converted into a bench type sofa thingy and would later become a bed for Henry, when I retired to his bedroom for the night.

'Hehh! Oh no! Not again, the bloody hiccups! Hehh! Must be this wine!' I blamed the wine entirely.

'Ah, not to worry, I think hiccups in a woman are kinda sexy,' Henry replied.

Well, I didn't quite know how to respond to that, so I didn't. And then there was silence. We both sat next to each other on Henry's tiny two-seater listening to my hiccups. Me in my marital disappointment and Henry in his... well, I didn't exactly know what was going through his mind. Although it wasn't long before I guessed. He reached his hand over to mine and held it.

'Hmmmm,' I said, feeling comfort from his touch.

'This is nice, isn't it, Beatrice? Just you and me, here now, in my caravan, isn't it?' He looked towards me. I could feel his eyes on me. I was thinking about how relieved I was that he could now pronounce my name properly, but I didn't want to embarrass him by drawing attention to it.

Then he'd realise that he was previously, pre front teeth installation that is, mispronouncing my name. I felt a bit awkward and didn't know what to do, so I picked up my wine and knocked a bit back. We were getting quite far through the second bottle. I wondered if he had another one in his miniature fridge. I took another sip, getting self-conscious now, as I was aware he was still looking my way. He sensed my unease.

'We have more work to do tomorrow morning before you leave. Do you want to call it a night? You can have my room, obviously,' he added. Then, more silence.

I thought about going home to Dublin the next day, but then realised I didn't want to leave. I wasn't ready. I felt safe here. With Henry. In his caravan.

I didn't feel prepared to face Jeffrey. Not yet. I didn't know what I would say to him. Would I tell him that I knew? I knew what he'd been getting up to behind my back. Would I unleash my rage upon him all at once or drip feed it to him over time? The latter would probably be more torturous for him in the long run, but I didn't think I'd be able to withhold my feelings like that. I wasn't sure. Maybe I'd wait and see how he behaved towards me on my return. I guess it would all depend on whether the kids were there or not. I looked down. We were still holding hands. I turned and looked towards Henry. He was leaning back now with his eyes closed. I was glad his eyes were shut and he was resting. It gave me a chance to study his face.

I noticed his voluminous eyelashes, voluptuous lips and sun-beaten, weathered skin. Jeffrey would never let his skin wear like that. He was SPF obsessed. His skin was smooth, naturally sallow and abundantly clear. Henry's was patchy, creased and rough to touch. Well, I imagined it would be, if I touched it, sometime. Like, maybe now.

I could touch it. He was very close to me, within reach. I thought about it but didn't act on it. My hand fell out of his and my eyes travelled lower, to his shoulders. He was lean and muscular with strong-looking shoulders. No doubt a natural result of intense manual labour, what with being a fisherman. Jeffrey's physique was a more sculpted one, as a result of working out in our home gym, which he always found time to fit into his busy working day. It occurred to me that he fit a heck of a lot into his daily schedule. Cooking for the family to sweeten us up, filling me with wine to dull my senses and turn a blind eye, while he hooked up with young, slim, tall, fashionable women in skinny jeans and tight blazers. The image of both of them laughing and talking like casual lovers on our doorstep (ON OUR DOORSTEP!) made me want to puke. How could he?

And what if the neighbours saw her slipping in

and out of the house? Had the man no shame? We lived in a tight-knit, family-oriented community. I mean, what must 81-year-old Mrs. Johnson next door think when she sees Jeffrey's latest bit on the side leaving our house when his wife of seven years is away on a...on a business trip. I put my head in my hands. Oh, what did I care what Mrs Johnson thought? I hardly ever saw her anyway, apart from the annual obligatory neighbours' Christmas drinks. I massaged my forehead, thinking I should really go to bed soon and get some sleep.

'Are you okay, Beatrice?'

'Oh! You gave me a fright!' I jumped. 'I thought you were asleep.'

'You look tired,' he said. 'Go on, head in there. I'll stay here.'

His head nodded towards me and our faces met. I think I was leaning in to say, 'thanks, yes, I am tired. I'll take your room.' And maybe he was just saying goodnight. I don't really know how it happened. I mean, I had the bones of a bottle of wine in me and probably the toxins left in my system from the two bottles yesterday. Not to mention venomous thoughts of my cheating husband swirling around in my brain. No, I don't know how it happened, but somehow our lips met. It was just a peck at first, but one of us came back for more. Or both of us? It was all a blur. We were like greedy woodpeckers and then it turned into full-on kissing, kind of like love-hungry teenagers.

Then he reached his hand upwards and touched my breast. Wow! I wasn't expecting that. This really was like teenage petting. I briefly made a mental note to check what age Henry was. I was confident he wasn't a teen, even though we were both acting like love-sick sixteen-year-olds. He continued feeling my breast, cupping and squeezing it through my clothes, until he worked up the nerve to go under my top. He was planning to go for it. I could tell. As he continued to stroke the bare skin on my back and tease out my bra strap, I wondered if I should reciprocate, although men don't have as many erogenous zones as us women, so there was really only one place I could go. And I wasn't prepared to go THERE!

I just sort of patted his back instead, as if to say, 'there, there, it's all going to be ok'. He tried to scooch closer to me and that's when my hand fell. Ahhh! (Internal scream!) What was that? Something hard. My hand touched something HARD. What was that? It was all happening so fast, too fast, way too fast, so I stopped.

'You okay, Beatrice?' Henry asked, somewhat alarmed at my withdrawal. I looked at him, deep into his ocean blue eyes.

'Jeremy betrayed you first. You've done nothing wrong,' he said. I closed my eyes and nodded, agreeing that he had a point. He was very reassuring. With that apt reminder of my double-crossing husband, we leaned in again and our kissing became more savage and passionate. His hand slid back under my top and he continued to set the pace of our relations. As his breathing got deeper, I suddenly remembered where my hand had fallen. OMG, it was still there, resting on a highly sensitive organ. I could feel it through his jeans. Alarm bells sounded between my ears and this time, I screamed aloud.

'Ahhh!' I exclaimed and pulled away immediately.

Henry got a fright and jumped back in terror. I gasped. What just happened? I asked myself, as I looked down at my culpable hand.

'I'm going to wash my hands,' I announced and excused myself from his company. I left Henry looking utterly bewildered on the two-seater. I went into the bathroom, thankful that there was no mirror. I didn't want to look at myself right now. I scrubbed my hands, went to the toilet and scrubbed them again. I exited the bathroom and side-stepped into the bedroom. I didn't look for him to join me. Then I closed the door, fell on the bed and passed out.

✧ ✧ ✧

THE NEXT MORNING, I was awoken by the smell of

fish. *Ouch! My head hurts.* Two consecutive morning hangovers was more than I'd had since the kids were born. I didn't have time to drink enough these days to achieve a hangover. Probably a good thing, I decided, as I dragged myself out of bed. Hangovers were not good and then, all of a sudden, I remembered the previous night's events. Ahhhhhhhhh! I looked down and admonished my blameworthy hand. How could you? I berated it. Oh God, what was I going to do now?

I put my ear to the door and heard the pan sizzling and then the kettle boiling. I couldn't escape from this matchbox without being noticed. I realised I'd have to face the music. I'd have to be professional about it. This was a business trip after all. 'Huhhhhhh!' I don't know if my desperate sigh was a laugh or a cry, but I felt something and felt it deeply and then pushed it into the pit of my tummy with a deep breath. Professional, I told myself. I must get this first leg of the project underway. I have work to do. I opened the bedroom door.

'Ah, good morning, Beatrice! You slept well in there! I'm sure I heard you snoring!'

'Oh no! Did you? I'm mortified! Sorry!' How embarrassing, I thought.

'Ah, don't be sorry, I think it's sexy when a woman snores!' he beamed, proudly.

'And hiccups too?' I remembered from last

night.

'Haha, yeah! That too! A hiccuping, snoring woman! You know, someone who can truly let go. I find it liberating!' He caught my eye and we both laughed. A little at first, but when I accidentally snorted mid chuckle, we laughed harder and louder.

'That too?' I asked, hardly able to get the words out.

'Yeah! Why not? Snorting, burping, farting, sure just let it all out! That's what I say!'

'Oh Henry, you're hysterical!' I acknowledged, relieved that there was no awkwardness between us.

Chapter Ten

A LITTLE MORE innuendo ensued when we both admitted we were ravenous and Henry assured me he had 'plenty of fish'. I raised my eyes and he gave up. We had some tomatoes and fried cod for breakfast. Like the hangovers, I'd never had so much fish in two consecutive days either, or at least, smelled so much fish. It was a strangely satisfying start to the day though, and we discussed the next section of the project. We planned out our morning, with only geography in mind. I filled in my survey, all my questionnaires and ticked every box in my folder. The first leg of the project was completed by two o'clock.

Henry asked if I wanted to get some lunch before I left, but I declined, insisting I'd grab something on the way. I packed up my bits and bobs from his caravan and we embraced warmly before I got into my car.

'Good luck with confronting Jeremy,' he said.

'Oh, it's Jeffrey, but thanks. Yeah, I don't know how I'm going to broach the subject, but I've a four-hour car journey to mull over it.' I smiled. 'Thanks, Henry, and I'll...well, I'm sure I'll be in touch. About the project, anyway.'

'Any more help you need, just give me a...well, you have my number and now, you know where I am.'

'Yeah, I do, em, thanks for everything.' Then I got in my car and drove off with a little knot in my stomach. I liked him, liked him a lot. But I also knew I could never come back here or see him again. After what happened between us. I just couldn't.

✧ ✧ ✧

MY FOOT ON the accelerator was getting sore and crampy. I'd driven so much in the last three days. More than I'd ever driven before. Usually for car journeys, Jeffrey did the driving and I sat in the passenger seat reading the latest edition of *National Geographic*. The kids demanded regular stops, so our journeys were always broken with picnics and toilet stops. My right foot was cramping badly and I cursed my Toyota for not having cruise control. I was starving anyway, so I pulled into a service station. I got some coffee and a chicken tikka panini. It gave me some much needed mental energy for the journey. Maybe now I could start figuring things out.

But I found I couldn't concentrate on my rage for Jeffrey. My mind kept redirecting me to Henry and our frantic encounter last night. I was still piecing it together in my brain. I just hadn't had any time yet to think about it properly. It shocked me to the core that it happened and yet thrilled me a little bit too. I was so glad he broke the ice this morning by being funny. It meant we could work together without awkwardness.

I also wondered if it made me a hypocrite and whether I'd have a leg to stand on when I confronted Jeffrey about his indecent fling. Would I tell him? I mean, who would it serve if I were to come clean? Jeffrey wouldn't need or want to know. Who would? And was it really such a big deal? It's not like I committed adultery or anything. Unless an accidental drop of the hand constitutes adultery? I wouldn't know. I was a bit out of touch, what with being a married person. How could I find out? Would Google know? I made a mental note to check later.

I wasn't trying to diminish what I did. I understood that, technically, I cheated on my husband, but if we were getting into technicalities, surely intercourse in the marital bed would be much further up the Richter Scale of Infidelities than an accidental, drunken fumble in a caravan. Wouldn't it? I suppose I did let him cop a feel of my breast though and that's fairly invasive. That ups the stakes considerably, I'd imagine. Not to mention the kissing and slobbering, although that was innocent in my mind. We simply lacked the language to say a polite goodnight to each other and got confused. Mixed messages led to the initial contact and then we just didn't want to let each other down by pulling back. We both really liked each other and wouldn't want to cause any mutual offence. I was upset enough about Jeffrey and...oh, yikes, I was making excuses for my behaviour. I was catching myself out. I couldn't go home and accuse Jeffrey of anything. Not after what I just did.

I turned on the radio to try to stop thinking. The guilt was getting to me. I sang along to an old favourite, 'Caravan of Love' by The Housemartins, but for some reason, that didn't help. It didn't make me feel better. My mind kept reverting back to recent events. Hmmm. If my memory serves me correctly, I stopped. When I eventually realised what was happening between me and Henry, I actually made the effort to pull away. It wasn't my fault that it went on a little longer than intended. I couldn't control how long it would take him to get aroused. In fact, I had no idea he was that hard until my hand accidentally dropped and felt it. His panting started fairly early on in our interaction, so it was unclear to me at which point he began to get carried away. If I had known, of course I would have stopped sooner. It's just that I got a bit excited too and lost track of time and I liked his hand on my... Oh, who am I kidding? This would never stand up in court. I'd let myself down, my family, my kids, my parents, Mr. Keel and the whole of the geography department. I was a failure.

Or...hang on a sec. Could I pin this fiasco on the sudden onset of a midlife crisis? I was forty years old after all, with no previous history of hysteria. Was this my 100k sports car moment? Or my brand new motorcycle parked in the driveway? Actually, they're more indicative of a man's midlife crisis. Maybe a woman of my age would get unnecessary and hugely expensive cosmetic surgery, or perhaps a young Italian lover or possibly become a secret shopper buying shoes or jewellery and going deep into debt. An innocent kiss in a colleague's caravan seemed pretty innocuous compared to... Oh, gosh, I couldn't seem to help myself. I was making excuses AGAIN and downgrading my indiscretion.

I thought I was going mad. I simply couldn't go on like this. I had to tell someone. But who? Jeffrey? Hmmm, park that thought for the moment. He was in my bad books and I didn't feel like opening up to him. My mum? Dad? Absolutely not. They'd kill me or call a doctor. They'd probably have me admitted into an institution if I relayed the events of this past weekend. No, not them. Jeffrey's parents? Nah, they loved me too much. They'd be too disappointed in me. I couldn't do that to them. My friend Cara? Hmmm. She'd been going through a tough time lately. And she might identify with the midlife crisis angle, since she was the same age as me. But, then again, she was never the most sensitive sort. She could be quite judgemental and that was the last thing I needed—I seemed to be doing a decent enough job of judging my own behaviour, and I didn't like it. Not one bit. No, Cara wasn't a suitable confidante for me. I thought of a few other friends and cousins, but found reasons against all of them. There was simply no one I could tell.

When I really thought about it, I realised the only people I felt comfortable opening up to, like really opening up to, were Jeffrey and Henry. Jeffrey was a great listener and always seemed concerned if my mood was low. And then, I suppose Henry was a revelation in that department. I revealed so much of my life to him over the past three days and he listened and responded adequately, without judgement. He was interested and sensitive and easy to talk to. It was a pity I'd never be seeing him again. I was going to miss him. His sense of humour and funny texts and… *Okay, that's enough.*

I was either going crazy or having an unexpected midlife crisis. Or both! That was the most likely explanation. Jeffrey's affairs were the triggers of course. I could completely blame him for my current situation. If he hadn't cheated on me, I would never have built up my expectations of Henry. I would have never allowed myself to get close to him. I would never have opened up to him or cried on his shoulder, because I would have had nothing to cry about, had Jeffrey not gone behind my back with other, younger women. And to think I'd forgiven him. The couple's counselling we did led me to forgive him for his affair with Linda. What kind of a mug was I? How many affairs had he had besides the two I knew about? I wouldn't be able to hold this in. I'd wait until the kids were in bed, obviously.

✧ ✧ ✧

I PULLED INTO our driveway and was struck by the colourful 'Welcome Home Mammy' poster plastered to the porch window. It was the first thing I saw. The kids were still up. I noticed the curtains upstairs hadn't yet been drawn. I took a deep breath and smiled. The kids were still up!

I badly needed their cuddles right now. I took another deep breath to prepare myself to see him. I needed to transition quickly into Mammy mode. Only joy and love were in my heart right now, as I turned the key in the front door.

'Mmmmmaaaammmmmmmmyyyyy!' Mia and Lauren heard me and raced into the hallway. They almost knocked me over with their exuberance. I relished every second of it and kissed them back twice as much as they kissed me. They wanted to know if I'd brought them presents back from my 'work holiday' as they called it. Luckily, I'd picked up some fluffy keyrings and a few bags of jellies at the last service station I'd stopped in. So glad I didn't forget, or they'd make me go back to Glan Mahogue to get them something!

Then, Jeffrey appeared with Daniel in his arms. He looked tired and I noticed Daniel's tear-soaked face. Sometimes the kids got the better of him too. He was only human. It looked as though it had been a fraught, demanding evening.

'Daniel!' I went over and took him from Jeffrey's arms for cuddles with Mammy. 'Hey, baby, what's up with you? Aren't you happy that Mammy's home? Look, I got you something!' I produced the furry dinosaur keyring for him and his face lit up. Myself and Jeffrey laughed when we saw his expression change so quickly. Then Jeffrey leaned in and pecked me on the cheek. 'Welcome home! We missed you! You must be exhausted after all that driving! How was it?'

I continued hugging Daniel in my arms. It felt good to hold on tight to my three-year-old. 'It was interesting and busy and yes, I'm wrecked.'

We all went into the kitchen and the girls showed me some more artwork they'd done, besides the lovely poster in the porch. They'd eaten already, but there was some spag bol left for me in the oven. Jeffrey got the kids ready for bed while I ate. I insisted on doing the bedtime story, though. I wanted to spend all my time with my children. I didn't wish to talk to Jeffrey. I just wanted to focus on the kids and that's what I did.

We read one of their favourites, *The Magic Moment*, and then I unpacked while they were nodding off. Jeffrey was cleaning up downstairs. I knew he was expecting me down for a chat about the weekend. While I was away, I'd spoken to him on Friday, but after that, I'd missed a couple of calls from him. I'd just texted back that I was in the middle of this or that and got reassurance that everything was okay. I hadn't wanted to talk to him after what I'd witnessed on Saturday morning. I knew he wouldn't be happy with me fobbing off his phone calls, but at this stage, I really didn't care.

Chapter Eleven

I WAS SURE I heard glasses clinking downstairs. He must have been expecting me to have a drink with him. I went down when I was ready and popped my head in the door.

'Jeffrey, listen, I'm wrecked after the trip. I badly need an early night, so I'm heading to...'

'There was no spa, was there?'

'Hmmm? What?' I asked.

'At the hotel.'

'What hotel?' He was confusing me.

'God, you ARE tired, Beatrice! I mean, I can see there was no spa at the hotel you stayed in, because your skin is very dehydrated.'

'It is?'

'You badly need a face mask, but look, you're weary now. Sleep is the best remedy for skin renewal. You're right to have an early night. Those dark circles will be gone by tomorrow if you get your eight hours.'

I reached my hand up to feel under my eyes. The skin on my face felt tight, as if it was swollen.

I instantly registered how disgusting I must look. Of course I looked gross. I'd literally had one of the most emotionally challenging weekends of my life. My self-care and beauty regime would have to wait until I recovered from the trauma. *Screw you Jeffrey Walsh for highlighting my flaws when I'm at my lowest ebb. I'll never forgive you for making me feel like this.*

'Listen, I can't wait to hear about your trip! I really can't! Tell me all tomorrow, won't you?' He came towards me to give me a hug before bed, but I didn't want one from him.

'Jeffrey, don't.' I stepped back. 'I stink, okay, after the long journey and well, I just really need to get some sleep.' I retreated and went upstairs, not even waiting to see his reaction.

I went into the bathroom to check my reflection. What was he talking about? And why did he make it sound so important? Yes, I was dry and dehydrated with dark circles under my eyes. Big deal! I'd just had a highly stressful weekend full of psychological turmoil, erratic driving, sleepless nights, countless bottles of medium quality white wine and an overabundance of fish. He was lucky I was still alive! How dare he pass comments on my appearance! The cheek of him. So what if I wasn't some fresh-faced, skinny twenty-year-old model! I was so much more than that. I was the mother of his children, his (up to recently) devoted wife, coearner and co-owner of our finances and beautiful house. *And I am, or I mean, WAS, his best friend.*

'Dark circles', 'dehydrated'… I'd show him. Just to spite him, I didn't even throw water on my face before bed. I didn't cleanse or tone or moisturise. I stared at myself in the bathroom mirror. It was abundantly clear I would no longer pander to Jeffrey's commands. I would take charge from now on. But first, I'd go and get my eight hours to rejuvenate. I stormed out of the bathroom, as quietly as I could, so as not to wake the kids.

✧ ✧ ✧

THE NEXT MORNING, I feigned a lie-in and waited for Jeffrey to leave with the kids for the school run. It was meant to be my day off anyway, so he wouldn't be expecting me to get up early. The minute the door shut, I jumped out of bed, had the quickest shower ever, including washing my itchy, greasy hair, and threw on some clean clothes. I pulled my hair back into a wet ponytail, slapped on some BB cream and when I saw how pale I looked, I slapped on some more. I legged it downstairs, grabbed my car keys and took off.

I just didn't want to face Jeffrey yet. At least, not first thing on a Monday morning. When I arrived at UCND, I realised Jeffrey must have arrived home by now, so I texted him that I'd been called into work to cover for a colleague. It wasn't a complete lie. I was at work after all, just by choice instead of at someone's behest. I wanted to tidy up my findings from the weekend. It was all a bit scribbled and rushed and handwritten. I intended to type it up and present it formally. I also wanted to do a little more research in the library to find the geology book Henry had mentioned. He kept alluding to it when we were out and about, so I couldn't wait to get my hands on it to cross reference all the facts I'd collected.

My phone beeped just as I was turning it to silent, before entering the library.

Jeffrey
Ah, that's a shame. I was hoping to hear all about your trip. Maybe tonight? I'm cooking that Goan fish curry and got that French Muscadet that you like, to accompany it

You two-faced pig, I thought. *I won't touch that wine in case it numbs my senses like you hope it will. You're trying to brainwash me with your culinary skills and talent for finding just the right wine to match every dish. It's abuse! Brainwashing is a form of mental abuse and I'll no longer succumb to your bait. You double-crossing, lying manipulator! When I think of how you pulled the wool over my eyes for so many years. How many years? I don't know. Were there others before*

Linda? Well, now I know there were definitely more since.

I tried to control my breathing. I decided not to enter the library just yet. I retreated into the corridor and stood with my back against the cold, hard, concrete wall. I reached my hand behind to feel it. Solid. Dependable. Smooth. It worked. It calmed me down. The university wall had saved me on so many occasions and it was working for me now. It grounded me and gave me courage to reply to his text with vengeance.

Beatrice
I had a lot of fish over the weekend

Slight delay with his reply. He must have needed time to process my hostile response, or something...

Jeffrey
Oh. Don't worry, I'll pack it with veg and I'll eat most of the fish. Would that work?

I sidled up closer to the wall and pressed my lower back against it. There was no one around, so I pressed harder and swayed from side to side, massaging my sacrum. Soothing. Very soothing. I sighed deeply.

Beatrice
I'm very busy

I knew he wouldn't like that reply. He would say I didn't make myself clear, but I didn't care. I left my trusty wall and went into the library, where I spent a few hours mulling over rock journals and tidying up my report. By 12 pm, I was starving as I'd only grabbed a coffee on my way in this morning. I went to the cafeteria and ordered salad and chips. I was just about to tuck in, when Mr. Keel spotted me and came over.

'Beatrice! I didn't expect to see you here today! Aren't you supposed to be recuperating after working all weekend?'

'Oh, hi Mr. Keel! Yes, I just popped in to finalise my findings. My notes were handwritten, so I typed them up in the library.'

He smiled his avuncular smile. 'You're a wonder! So dedicated! You know, you have until the end of the week to do that. We're meeting on Friday, isn't it?'

'Yes, Friday at 10.'

'How did you get on in the west, Beatrice?'

'Em, yes, good. It was very informative.'

'I hope you had time to enjoy yourself while you were there. It wasn't all work and no play, was it?'

Gulp. I coughed. 'Oh sorry, I think there's some lettuce stuck in my throat. Yes, I, em, briefly managed to soak up the local atmosphere.' I broke eye contact with him when I acknowledged to myself that the atmosphere I soaked up was mainly in Henry's caravan.

'And how did your contact work out for you? The fisherman, Henry something or other?'

I coughed again. For longer this time. 'Oh yeah, we made contact…' I didn't know what to say.

'And?'

'Ahem, yes, great local knowledge. And very approachable.'

'Was he a suitable choice to help out with the study, in your opinion? You know, we need to be careful about who we let in. This is a private university project, after all. It's privileged information when you think about it.'

'Hmm, yes, well I think we can trust him.' *I bloody hope I can.* 'He's enthusiastic about sharing his knowledge. He was a good choice to include in the research side of things. He knows the area really well.'

'Great! I'll add him to the list. We may need more input from him in the future. Don't forget to credit him in your acknowledgements. Sorry, I'm sure you won't, Beatrice.'

I smiled in reply, willing him to stop talking about Henry. Then he smiled back and raised his brow.

'And tell me, did you dip your hand in?' he asked, playfully. Did he really just say that?

My hand? Why was he asking about my hand?

Did he know what I did with my hand in Henry's caravan? Could it be obvious this hand was involved in extra marital, extra curricular affairs? I scanned the cafeteria with panic stricken eyes. Did I accidentally include the whole sorry saga in the project? Did Henry ring him and alert him? Or did I just simply have a very guilty-looking hand right now? There'll be no hiding it if that's the case. Or could there possibly have been cameras in Henry's caravan? Was I viral now? Did everybody know? I looked around.

'Beatrice, are you alright? Have I upset you? I just meant, did you dip your toe in the water? You know, into the cold Atlantic while you were there?'

'Oh my God, right! You said TOE! Not HAND! Sorry, I misheard you completely! Did I dip my toe in the water? I see what you mean! Hahahahaha!' Was I going mad? I held that thought for a moment.

He remained standing there, waiting for my response.

'Em, no. No, I didn't. Too cold.' I shrugged. Of course I didn't. I wasn't a crazy person! I wasn't one of those thrill-seeking sea swimmers, who risked their lives on a regular basis FOR NO APPARENT REASON! I mean, I thought Mr. Keel knew me better than that, but obviously not.

I finished my salad and was thinking about going home. Jeffrey would probably be holed up in his office and most likely not notice me slipping in and tiptoeing up to our room. I just wanted to have a nap. The exhaustion from the past few days was catching up on me. I needed a few hours to myself and then, hopefully, I'd be able to face Jeffrey and have some sort of a conversation with him later that evening. I couldn't avoid him forever.

✧ ✧ ✧

MY PLAN WORKED, or so I thought. There was no movement in the kitchen, so I assumed he was out in the extension, which he used as his office. I relaxed a bit and filled a glass of water to bring upstairs. I slipped off my shoes and turned my phone to silent in the hallway. I didn't think there was anything else I'd need, so I made my way upstairs feeling my feet cushioned by the soft carpet beneath. I couldn't wait to melt into bed and hide away for a few hours. It really had been the most taxing weekend. THE MOST I'd had in a long time, or possibly ever.

I opened our bedroom door and immediately dropped my glass of water, as I registered the sight before me.

'Ahhhhhhh!' I screamed.

'Ahhhhhhhh!' Jeffrey screamed back.

I retreated, lost my footing and stumbled. Who

was this person before me? He looked as terrified as I felt. I could see it in his panic-stricken eyes. His brown eyes—they were the one feature of his that I recognised. I knew it was him, even though it wasn't really him. Not my husband at all.

'Jeffrey! What on earth are you...? What the hell is going on?'

He put his hand to his heart in what seemed like an effort to circumvent a heart attack. 'Beatrice! What are you doing at home? I thought...I thought you were working today?'

'Hang on a sec. You don't get to question me right now. I'm not the one who has to answer to you. What the heck?' I started to panic and my breathing quickened. 'What the heck, Jeffrey?' I started to cry. He stood there, looking at me with wide, sorrowful eyes. He saw how shocked and upset I was. This was the last thing in the world I was expecting. It made no sense to me at all.

Chapter Twelve

MY HUSBAND WAS standing in our bedroom with a full face of makeup. And I don't just mean some liner and mascara or a hint of lippy. I'm talking about a thick, heavy foundation caked onto his face, with painted eyebrows and about six layers of blusher plus the same number of colours in his eyeshadow.

'Jeffrey! Is that...? Is that contouring?'

He wasn't quite sure what to say and he looked down. Then, I looked down too and saw the cases of makeup that lay by his feet. Expensive, branded makeup by the looks of it. He didn't just pop out to *Dealz*. He had all the high-end brands and the designer bags to go with them. I even noticed a red and white striped one from *Bella Mae*. I was utterly perplexed.

'Jeffrey, you need to start talking to me. NOW!'

'Beatrice, I can explain all of this. I promise. And it's not what you think, so don't start jumping to conclusions, right?'

'Don't you dare tell me what I can or cannot do! You don't dictate what goes on in my head!' Suddenly, the exhaustion I'd felt turned to anger. It was building. Who was this man? Who did I marry? What the hell was going on?

'Okay, Beatrice. I can see that you're angry. Look, I don't want to explain everything looking like this. Can I just go and take this off my face and meet you downstairs in, say, 15 minutes? Please?'

I didn't want to talk to him looking like that either, so I picked up my empty glass and went downstairs. I took some painkillers and lay on the couch. I could hear the tap on at full blast and imagined the scrubbing he would have to do to remove those layers of makeup. My mind wouldn't work due to the onset of a throbbing headache and I couldn't fathom how he was going to explain this. I couldn't predict where it would go. I knew nothing. I rubbed my forehead in efforts to soothe myself. 'What was happening?' I whispered to myself and then heard his footsteps approaching.

I sat up when he entered the living room.

'Beatrice, I'm so sorry you saw me like that. What a terrible shock to get. It's not something you see every day.'

'Don't you dare make light of this, Jeffrey!' I warned him.

'No, no I'm not. Not at all. Em, I think I need a

drink. Do you want one?'

'No! Don't try to get me drunk before you explain yourself! That won't work anymore! I'm onto you now!' I narrowed my eyes.

'Em, I don't really know what you mean, but I need a stiff drink.'

He went to the cupboard and poured himself a whiskey. I started to get worried. What was he going to tell me? And why did he need Dutch courage? I felt weak and was glad I was sitting down. He pulled a dining chair over and sat opposite me. I noticed his hair was still wet after washing his face. His skin was shining. If anyone else had to scrub that much makeup off, their skin would be dry and flaking, but not Jeffrey's. It was glistening. I even noticed it sparkle. I considered that maybe there'd been glitter in his eyeshadow.

'Beatrice, you know how you've embarked on the communications course?'

'Jeffrey! This isn't about me!'

'Hear me out, hear me out.' He took a deep breath. 'I was impressed that you would take an evening course to upskill and...'

'Jeffrey, it wasn't my choice. I had to, or I may have lost my job.'

'Yes, yes, I know you were advised to do it. But it got me thinking about personal development and I, well, I started looking into courses that I could do. I subscribed to MasterClass online, so I could get a taste of different classes that I might like to try. There's a huge range, like cookery, sport, music, gardening... Well, there's actually something to suit everyone. But when I scrolled through them all, I realised I could narrow down my interests fairly easily.'

'So what? You chose cookery, right? That's your hobby, you always say you love cooking.'

'Yes, yes I do love cooking, but I'm at the stage now where I know what I'm doing in the kitchen and I really don't need to do a class. I experiment with flavours and dip in and out of cookbooks. Look, no, a cookery course didn't appeal to me, so...'

'What about DIY? I'd love it if I didn't have to call a handyman every time something breaks around the house.'

He took a slug of whiskey and laughed a little. 'No, DIY didn't jump out at me either.'

Silence ensued. I checked my watch. I didn't want us accidentally forgetting to collect the kids.

He peered at me with his abundantly clear, brown eyes. 'Makeup,' he said, earnestly. 'It was fashion photography and makeup artistry that caught my eye.' He leaned back in his chair. 'I've always had an interest in skincare, Beatrice. I know I haven't shared it with you over the years, but it's been a quiet passion of mine. I suppose I inherited it from my mother. And then I guess the interest in makeup grew from there. You know, sometimes when you have your early nights, I watch *Ireland's Next Top Model* and shows like that. I've learned a lot from them and followed the MasterClass. Then, I started another face-to-face makeup application course in Ballyfermot.'

'Ballyfermot? When do you go there?' I was in shock. That was miles away.

'Every Wednesday morning from 10 until one. There's a beauty school there and the times suited me.'

'But your job, Jeffrey? You have a full-time job!' I tried to bring him back to reality.

'I told you the recent projects that have come up are way beneath me and I can manage the workload in a four-day week, no bother. So, I dedicate every Wednesday and the odd afternoon when things are slow, like today, to pursuing my dream.'

'Hey, hey, steady on now. Your dream?' He was moving way too fast for me.

'Yes, my dream of being a professional makeup artist and/or fashion photographer, but hopefully both in tandem if I do everything right.'

'Okay, Jeffrey, I think I WILL have a whiskey.' He fetched me one and I thanked him earnestly. The painkillers weren't doing much for my headache, but maybe this would.

'Look, with my communications course, I'm

not chasing my dreams or anything. It's a means to an end. I'm doing it so I can continue my real job and become better at it. What I'm saying is, you already have a real job. You don't need to pursue any fantastical dreams.'

His shoulders dropped. 'Oh, I was hoping you wouldn't see it like that. I've been doing IT consultancy since I left uni, and granted, it has always paid the bills, and then some, but it has never actually fulfilled me. I don't get that sense of satisfaction that you seem to get from your geography research. Does that make sense?'

'Well, I've noticed you don't rave about your job as much as I do mine, but I always thought it didn't matter, because it freed up time for you to look after the kids and cook family meals and...'

'Don't get me wrong. I deeply appreciate having the time to do those things, but I'm only forty and I don't want to give up on my...'

'Oh, I see. It's another midlife crisis! Like the one you had two years ago when you had an affair. It's happening again and you're going to blame it all on your midlife crisis, aren't you? And then expect me to forgive you, just like last time. Is that it?'

With that, he got up and grabbed the keys.

'Where are you going?' I demanded.

'To collect the kids,' he hollered back.

'But, it's only 4.30,' I said.

'I know, but I can't drive after the whiskey, can I? And neither can you. I'll have to walk. It'll take at least a half hour. I need the fresh air anyway, to clear my head. See you later.'

And just like that, he was gone. I was left on the couch with half a glass of whiskey that I didn't want. I drank it regardless, because I didn't know what else to do with it. He was gone to get the kids.

Dinner. What would we have for dinner? Did he have something in mind? I didn't know. I could have walked over to the fridge to check, but I lay back on the couch instead. That was a lot of information to process and I still had many unanswered questions. I sighed and closed my eyes. Life was so exhausting these days.

✧ ✧ ✧

I WOKE UP after an hour and they still weren't home, so I washed the whiskey glasses and stuck a few frozen pizzas in the oven. I guess it was a longer walk back with two five-year-old girls who liked to stop and pick flowers and a three-year-old that would refuse to walk and most likely end up on his daddy's shoulders.

I wanted to sit down and have a think about Jeffrey's revelations, but just as the pizzas were ready, they arrived home.

'What's for dinner?' Lauren enquired.

'Pizza!' I exclaimed.

'Oh, so Mammy cooked today,' Mia announced. That hurt a little and I locked eyes with Jeffrey. He smiled, sympathetically. We got through the mayhem of dinner and I gave Daniel a quick and much overdue bath before bed. I read him a story and Jeffrey put the girls to bed. Then, it was just the two of us downstairs in the kitchen. We made some small talk while cleaning up and Jeffrey asked if we could continue our chat from earlier. I don't know why, but I felt nervous. All that had seemed so familiar to me now felt rather foreign and I didn't like the uncertainty. I poured a glass of red to settle my nerves and joined him in the living room.

'Thanks for collecting the kids. I forgot we wouldn't be able to drive because of the whiskey.'

'Yeah, that's okay. I think you were accusing me of having a midlife crisis before I left.'

'Yeah, I believe that's where we left it.'

'I'm sorry you're still thinking about my affair. I suppose it's only natural that it's still on your mind. I don't think about it anymore, just if you ever wonder. I left it all behind at the couple's counselling and I don't go back there. I assumed you did the same as me, but I guess it's harder for you to forget, isn't it?'

I put my head down. 'Yes, it still hurts and now

I find you're doing more stuff behind my back.'

'I can assure you I'm not hiding stuff like that from you. Maybe you're right, it was a midlife crisis then, but now I don't think this is. It's more like midlife enlightenment. You see, I know the direction I want and I've started the ball rolling to get there. This is going to fulfil me and if I don't do it now, I never will. I don't want to regret not trying, Beatrice. Do you understand?'

'No, no, I don't think I do.' I was waiting for him to confess he was into younger women and I was too old and wrinkly for him, but he kept focussing on his career. That was all he wanted to talk about. He continued.

'It would be like if you decided not to take Mr. Keel's advice about the communications course. And let's say, five years pass and you're struggling to get your curriculum across to your students and they're failing or dropping the subject of geography. Wouldn't you wonder then if things might be different had you agreed to do the course? You might regret not doing it or consider starting it, having wasted the last five years. You see, I don't want that to happen to you. I want you to do the course and learn from it and improve, so you'll enjoy your daily grind at university all the more, because you've developed and upskilled. I want it for you and I want it for me too. I don't want to look back and say, 'I wish I did it then, when I had the time.' Things change and move fast in the IT world and if I don't take advantage of this 'slow' period now, I might never get it again. You know how my projects change every six months. Who knows how demanding the next one will be?'

'Okay, okay, do the course, but what then? Are you going to quit your day job? Where does that leave us financially?' I asked.

'No, I won't do anything to jeopardise the finances of our family. I won't make any rash decisions either. Whatever I do, I'll discuss it with you first. I promise.'

He needed to hear a home truth, so I gave him one.

'I don't trust you, Jeffrey'.

Chapter Thirteen

'BEATRICE! WHY WOULD you say that?' He seemed hurt.

I paused. Should I tell him that I saw her? I saw her leaving our house on Saturday morning. I wasn't sure how to communicate the fact that I knew she'd been here. It was such a long story that started with my disappointment about Henry being shorter than I'd imagined and considerably gummier. No, I couldn't go there now. I couldn't get into all that at this hour on a Monday night. A school night. But I did offer him an alternative answer.

'You didn't discuss the makeup course with me. You didn't confide in me about any of it, until I caught you today. And, by the way, you haven't explained that situation earlier to me yet.'

'Okay, fair enough. I didn't confide in you about the MasterClass or the weekly course I'm doing. I guess I saw how busy you were and under stress after that talk with Mr. Keel. I was sort of waiting for the right time. I wanted to try it out for a few weeks to make sure it was right for me. There was always a chance I'd pack it in if I didn't like it, but turns out I absolutely LOVE it and want to weave my way into that world, somehow.'

'Is that all you want to tell me, Jeffrey?'

'What...what do you mean, Beatrice? Isn't that enough?'

I took a deep breath. 'I'm a bit tired. I think I'll go and read and hit the sack. I've my course tomorrow evening, so I'll be late home, okay?'

'Yeah, I know, that's okay. Are you okay? You seem a bit...oh, you asked me to explain my actions in the bedroom earlier. I was just trying out contouring. I'd been watching lots of tutorials on YouTube and we're covering it in class next week, so I thought I'd experiment and well, as I said, it was a slow afternoon, workwise.'

'Lock the door next time. You'll frighten the children.' I handed him my empty glass and went to bed. My phone beeped on my way upstairs.

Henry
How are you, Beatrice? Did you have it out with Jeremy yet?

Oh, he was texting now. I thought we'd said goodbye and left it at that unless I needed him for the project. Should I answer? Did I want to engage with him? I knew I liked him, but it would feel weird remaining friends with him. I'd inadvertently touched his private parts and he'd touched approximately 20% of mine, ballpark guesstimate, albeit through my clothing. That wasn't something you'd do with your friends, was it? Especially not if one of them was married. No, I'd ignore his text, even though I wanted to correct him and say, it's Jeffrey not Jeremy, but I didn't. I didn't reply. Probably for the best.

Later that night, I turned on my side and feigned slumber when Jeffrey got into bed. I still didn't trust him. He wasn't telling me everything. I wondered when or if he was planning to come clean. I hated having these familiar feelings of distrust surface again. It reminded me of how I felt when I found out about Linda. I dreaded the idea of having to go through all that again. I had really put my faith into the promises he'd made at marriage counselling, but events of late made it abundantly clear that my husband was incapable of keeping promises.

✧ ✧ ✧

'GOOD VERBAL COMMUNICATION means saying just enough—don't talk too much or too little. Try to convey your message in as few words as possible. Say what you want clearly and directly.'

We had been given a manual for the communications course, but I still scribbled furiously, especially when something the facilitator said rang true for me. I realised that sometimes my lectures were very wordy, as I endeavoured to include every last detail about the topic in question. But now it was making sense to me that being concise was key. I was losing students with too much information. I needed to convert my lecture notes into bullet points and prioritise the key information. They didn't need to know absolutely everything. They could absorb the lesser relevant course material when they were studying by themselves. It wasn't necessary for me to spoon-feed them. This was a revelation to me and I skipped out of the classroom hugging my newfound scribbled wisdom to my chest.

I had a lot to do over the next day or two, as we were due to have our first practical on Thursday evening, where we had to do a ten-minute presentation to the group and include all the methodologies we'd learned thus far. I was excited about the challenge, despite others in the class looking seriously daunted. Many of them were younger than me and most were not from teaching backgrounds. I'd been a bit embarrassed admitting that I was a university lecturer, but no one seemed to bat an eyelid or query how I found myself there. They didn't question why I needed lessons in communication, given I communicated information daily to lecture halls of students. I had vast experience and really should have been facilitating the course rather than participating in it. However, I didn't get the impression that anyone else cared. No one seemed to be judging me, apart from myself.

✧ ✧ ✧

WHEN I GOT home that night, I received another text from Henry.

> Henry
> Well, Beatrice, any news?

I held back. I still didn't want to engage with him. Maybe I'd have something to share with him after my meeting with the rock study team on Friday.

Jeffrey was in the mood for chats too. He gave me some free samples he'd received with makeup orders and I thanked him, even though I didn't know how or when to apply a beauty luminizer or a restorative resurfacer. I accepted them nonetheless and assumed at some stage he'd explain what I should do with them.

I shared details with him regarding my upcoming assessment and let him know I'd be studying for the next few days. He looked a little lost and forlorn, as if he was lonely or something. Maybe he wanted to open up to me about his latest affair but thought better of it when he heard how busy I was. I couldn't work it out, but whatever it was, it would have to wait until my assessment was out of the way.

✧ ✧ ✧

'AND THAT, MY friends and comrades, concludes how Mammatus clouds are formed. Any questions and/or feedback?'

I beamed angelically at my classmates and course facilitator. I almost did a twirl on completion, so pleased was I with my performance. I honestly felt it couldn't have gone any better. I also knew I had a distinct advantage over my classmates in the sense that low self-esteem, confidence and anxiety were major stumbling blocks for them. However, being an experienced lecturer, I didn't suffer from a lack of self-belief. My main obstacle was trying to rein it in and only divulge the necessary information in a clear, concise fashion. I knew clarity was a failing of mine. Even Jeffrey complained that I never replied to his text messages with a straightforward answer. He had to text numerous times to confirm my reply. It was a bugbear of his. I was guilty of that.

I rang him as I approached the car park. I wasn't going to let our current relationship woes cloud my professional successes. 'Stick the bubbly in the freezer. Cause for celebration!' He did as requested and luckily the kids were asleep by the time I got home, just before nine o'clock. I didn't want a serious conversation about our marriage tonight. I wanted to toast my amazing performance this evening. A win in communications for me was a victory for geography in UCND in the long run!

'Guess what?'

'What? Tell me what we're celebrating!' He looked excited and delighted for me.

'Take a look. My first practical assignment. Top of the class! Ninety two percent! See, look here. "*Vocal Impact—Very Strong; Body Language—Highly Effective; Engagement With Audience—Impactful; Ability To Create And Maintain Rapport—Strong*". Isn't that marvellous, Jeffrey?'

'Wow, tremendous! And look what it says here about voice.'

'Oh, yeah? What was my result there? I can't remember.'

'It says, "*Presenter's Voice—Abundantly Clear*".'

High praise. High praise indeed. I felt elated.

'Cheers!' And our glasses clinked.

'You look chuffed with yourself, Bea! Well done!'

'I am, thanks. This means so much to me and I

know it will help me longterm and make me a more effective lecturer. Mr. Keel knew what he was doing when he recommended this course. I've so much to thank him for. I mean, he could have sacked me, considering the number of complaints he'd received from students.'

'Nah, he has too much respect for you. He knew you just needed a little boost. Further education at our age is really the way to go. You know in your teens and twenties, you just don't really know what you want and you go with the flow and do what's expected of you. But, now, in our forties, we've been there, done that and we're more experienced. We know what it is we want and further ed is a means of getting there. That's why we take it so seriously, unlike your geography students, who don't seem to know what the hell they want to do with their lives.'

I thought about what he said. He was an eloquent communicator. He could always get his point across. He never would have needed a communications course. 'Yes, that makes sense, Jeffrey.'

'I'm just so glad that you know. You know what your passion is and you're going for it with gusto.' Then he put his head down and looked sad. 'At least one of us is succeeding,' he muttered.

I reached out, instinctively, and touched his arm. 'Oh, Jeffrey, I didn't realise you were so unhappy. Isn't the makeup course doing it for you?'

'It is and I love it. I just don't feel like I have your support. I know you found me in a compromising position in our bedroom the other day and that's not how I wanted to share my new venture with you. I wanted to sit down with you and have a heart-to-heart, but you were in shock after discovering me with makeup on, and I don't...I don't think you were capable of being receptive.'

'I was exhausted after an unbelievably busy weekend. In fact, you wouldn't believe how tumultuous it was! I was actually going into the bedroom for a nap and you caught me by surprise.'

'I know. I know I did and I'm sorry. I didn't hear you coming. I thought that after you had time to process the shock, you might show more interest, but you never asked me how my contouring class went yesterday morning. You don't seem like you're rooting for me the way I am for you.'

Of course I'm not. I can't trust you. I checked my watch and it was nearly 11 pm. I had that meeting the next morning where I'd be presenting the first leg of my rock study. I needed a good night's sleep.

'Jeffrey, I'll think about what you're saying. I promise I will. Maybe we'll have that heart-to-heart tomorrow evening. I just need to get to bed now. I've that meeting with Mr. Keel and the geography team and...'

He got up and took the champagne flutes to wash them. None of our crystal glasses were dishwasher safe. 'I know you do. You have another busy day. Yeah, we'll have that chat tomorrow. That's good.'

Why was I the one feeling guilty? He looked incredibly sad and dejected. Maybe he was worried about having to tell me the real truth about his sordid affair with a smoker. I imagined he must be feeling deep-seated shame about the whole fiasco. I knew I wouldn't like to be in his shoes right now. At least, I only had an innocent misunderstanding in a caravan to feel guilty about. And even that was fairly blameless in the sense that I ejected myself from the entanglement as soon as it got close to fever pitch. I removed myself and my fallen, limp hand. How was I to know Henry would get so aroused so quickly? I mean, how on earth could I know that? We were just smooching like teens, that was all. Jeffrey, on the other hand, had a second, INTENTIONAL affair to contend with. His heart must be so full of lies and deceit. I could understand why he looked so forlorn.

'Tomorrow, okay? I promise. We'll talk about everything then. Goodnight.' I gave him a little hug and a squeeze, only imagining how tortured his guilty soul must be right now.

Chapter Fourteen

I WAS GLAD I went to bed when I did. I needed all the energy I could summon to get through my rock study presentation. I used my new communicative skills and found I was smiling and making a lot more eye contact than usual. Mr. Keel seemed impressed and continued to smile back.

'Beatrice! Amazing! Well done! It makes me want to go and visit Glan Mahogue myself. Sounds like a hidden gem, tucked away so far west. Did you fall in love with the place?'

'I did! The wild, expansive beach took my breath away. Honestly, it's a must see.'

'And Henry provided vital local info, didn't he? It's great to have someone so knowledgeable on board! If only we had a Henry for every project!' He laughed and we all joined in, although my laughter was tinged with deep-seated nerves. I was ready to stop talking about Henry McCormack. I wanted to focus on other things now.

'Very handy, wasn't he, Beatrice? Very handy to have him on board,' Mr. Keel proclaimed.

Okay, okay enough already, with the 'handiness'. Please stop! You have no idea where his hand actually was. I instinctively checked that the buttons on my blouse were securely fastened, before smiling and nodding back with as much professionalism as I could muster.

'Hmm, yes, indeed. I better go now and get some lunch before my two pm lecture. See you all on Monday.' I was dying to get out of there. My phone beeped on my way to the cafeteria.

Henry
Any plans for the weekend, Beatrice? You're always welcome here in Glan Mahogue, you know that, don't you?

Oh, God, there were too many people pulling out of me. Henry was persistent, that was for sure. I hoped my lack of engagement wasn't hurting his feelings too much. He didn't deserve to get hurt in all of this. Although, he knew what he was doing, getting involved with a married woman. He went there, so he shouldn't expect it to be plain sailing after that. My life was getting complicated, though. I was looking forward to getting home early this evening and bringing the kids to their swimming lessons. The mayhem of that would ground me and then, hopefully, I'd be ready to receive whatever it was that Jeffrey wanted to share.

✧ ✧ ✧

'HEY, THIS IS nice to chill out and relax, isn't it? I thought Friday would never come!' Jeffrey kicked back on the couch and sipped the Cosmopolitan he'd just made. He made one for me too. When he was in college, he'd done an evening mixology course. This was another reason why my mum thought he was the perfect catch. '*An amazing cook AND he can whip up a cocktail at the drop of a hat. Sure, what more would you want?*' She was quite partial to a pina colada and insisted Jeffrey made a better one than the swankiest cocktail bar in Dublin.

'Did you feel it was a long week, Jeffrey? Are you under pressure now with the kids and housey stuff alongside the makeup course?' I wondered if it was all too much for him. He was looking kind of tired these days.

'Yeah, it's busy alright, but I wouldn't have it any other way. I love being able to take care of the kids when you're at work. One of the best things we've done this year was to sign up with that cleaning firm. It's not always the same cleaner, but she comes every Monday morning, and in three hours, the house is spotless. That really takes the pressure off. I'm coping well with the day job. It's a no-brainer project, but it frees up lots of time for me at the moment.'

'It all sounds great. You've got the time to devote to your newfound passion, then?'

'Yeah, I wanted to discuss something with you actually.' He took another sip, as did I. Here it comes, I thought. He was going to land the bombshell on me now. He was going to tell me that he'd found a new girlfriend. A new, younger, skinnier model with shinier hair than mine. How was her hair so shiny, anyway? She was a smoker. Smokers are supposed to have dry hair and dull skin and she had neither. Maybe that would come with age. *One can only hope...*

'I think I mentioned the fashion photography, didn't I?' he said.

'The what?'

'You see, I really want to freelance and be my own boss, so I'd not only do the makeup, but also be responsible for the all-important shot too. Does that make sense?'

What about the skinny-jeaned, tight-blazered beanpole escaping from our house last Saturday morning? 'Em, yes it does, Jeffrey.' I answered, knocking back more of my cocktail.

'Oh good, good. I was hoping you'd see the bigger picture and appreciate me projecting long term into the future.

'Mmhmm,' I murmured and drained my Cosmo.

'So, yeah, on Monday and Wednesday evenings, there's a part-time fashion photography certificate course beginning and I know it's a big ask, what with your Tuesday/Thursday communications course, but I wanted to get your blessing before I sign up for it. Now, it's not cheap and it's two evenings a week in the city centre, so it's a bit of upheaval for the family, but Beatrice, it's an integral component of me achieving my dream career.'

He looked at me wide-eyed, like a little boy asking his mother for the latest Batman toy. I stared back at him, deep into his eyes, searching for deceit, but I couldn't find any. He stood up. 'Oh, you need another one. I'll be back.' He took my glass and went to make me a fresh cocktail. I hung my head back and sank deeper into the couch. Hmmm...two evenings a week. She must have an apartment in the city centre and this was his ruse, so I wouldn't be suspicious when he slips away two nights a week to have sex with her. What was it Henry had called him? '*A double-crossing, two-faced shleeveen.*' I pulled out my phone and texted him.

> Beatrice
> Thanks for your messages, Henry, and all your help with the project. Yes, I will most certainly come back to visit you in Glan Mahogue. Yes, indeed I will!

Jeffrey came back and handed me my cocktail. *Hah! Trying to get me drunk, so I'll blindly accept his suggestions.*

'Who are you texting?' he asked.

'What? Who? Me? Cara. I'm texting Cara.'

'Cara Cawley? You two are back in touch. That's nice. Does she still wear that thick, heavy, black mascara?'

'Yes.' I had no idea.

'Shame,' he said and shook his head. 'It does her no favours. So, anyway, what are you thinking? Is it a goer or too much pressure on the family if I'm gone two nights a week?'

'Is the family REALLY your primary concern?' I asked with a hint of scepticism. Then, my phone beeped. Not once or twice, but roughly about six times. Oh no, I must have excited Henry. The prospect of me coming to visit had set him off. Yikes! I ignored the pinging.

'Of course! Always! Our family is always my primary concern.' I raised my eyes to heaven and he clocked it. 'Oh, you're still thinking about the affair, aren't you?' he said. 'Yes, it definitely wasn't my top priority then. I put myself first and it was selfish.' He put his head down in his hands. He was making me feel bad now for bringing it up. I wasn't supposed to feel bad! He was the one who had the affair! Not me! Not yet, anyway. *'Ping!' There goes my phone again.*

'Jeffrey, is there anything ELSE you want to tell me? Like, now that we're having this heart to heart... Anything?'

He looked up and seemed as though he was trying to think. 'Emmm, no, no I don't think so.' My heart sank. He wasn't going to confess anything to me tonight. Damn it! This would drag on and on. It would torture me. I'd rather deal with it now. *Will I say something? Will I tell him I saw her? Will I ask him if she slept in our bed?* She didn't have an overnight bag with her—did she use my towel or cleanser? Our shower gel? I had so many questions!

'Oh, by the way, Beatrice, there's a model calling tomorrow morning at nine am for a practical, okay? All my stuff is in my office, so I'll do her face in there. Tell the kids I have a meeting, so they won't barge in. Is that okay with you?'

'A what? What did you just say?' My stomach churned. The cocktail was coming back up.

'A model. You can hire them from the agency for an hour and if you're participating in the makeup course, you get a reduced rate because they subsidise it. It's really quite reasonable. I've done it before.'

'You...you have? When?' I couldn't breathe.

'Em, let's see. It was while you were in Glen Minogue. Emmm, last Saturday morning.' Oh, Lord and the shepherds and angels in heaven above! What have I done? My revenge sexual indiscretion was for nothing. For nothing! I looked down at my hand. My right hand. The one that slipped and accidentally touched Henry's... The guilty one. It was shaking. Jeffrey noticed. He took my Cosmo from me.

'Are you okay, Beatrice? Is this going to be a problem? It will only take an hour. I just have to get a before and after photo and send it off to my course facilitator. Honestly, she'll be gone by 10 o'clock.'

'Ahem, will she?' I was finding it difficult to catch my breath.

'Yeah, actually, I hope they send the same girl as last week. She was brilliant, so easy to work with. She's studying marketing in UCND and models part-time to earn a crust. I told her you worked there, but she hadn't heard of you. None of her friends study geography.'

'Hmmm, don't they? Hmmm.' I was trying to hide my internal panic. Badly.

'Beatrice, are you okay? Can I get you a glass of water? Is it that you're not happy with my choice of career change? I was worried about telling you. I suppose it's always been a secret passion of mine. I should have shared it with you sooner. I should have... Is that your phone again? Is it Cara? She's texting a lot, isn't she? Is she okay?' He looked concerned. He was so nice, showing concern for a friend of mine that he didn't even really like. I didn't much like her either, but we were old friends and hadn't gotten around to making any new ones yet. God, he was so considerate, looking at me wide-eyed, worried about my friend.

'Em, well, it's not just Cara texting.' I took my glass back and sipped more Cosmo. 'No, it's sort of a combination of her and Henry.' I looked down and checked my phone. Eight messages from Henry. 'But mainly Henry,' I admitted.

'Who's he?'

'Oh! I thought I told you. He was my contact in Glan Mahogue. For the project. He's a local fisherman.'

'No. No, you never mentioned him. I'd remember a name like Harry.'

'It's Henry.'

'Right. And is he stressing you out or something? You seem a bit off tonight.' He touched my hand. Ahhhh! The naughtly one. My right hand. He gave it a little squeeze. Oh no! I've been such an idiot. He's not a shleeveen at all. He's my kind, handsome, ambitious, perfect, loving husband. What will I do? *Ping*.

'Do you want to check that, Beatrice? In case there's something wrong.' *Noooooo, there's nothing wrong. It's just Henry sending me flirty texts and no, I don't want to check. I really don't.*

Chapter Fifteen

I WISH I'D never met Henry McCormack. I wish I'd never set eyes on his shorter-than-average frame and his toothless, gormless grin. I wish I'd never set foot in his crusty, old rusty caravan and I wish I hadn't let him seduce me on the dinner table that converts into a rock-hard, way-too-small-to-get-comfy two-seater. I wanted to cry. I wanted to and I did. I started crying. I couldn't help it.

'Bea, Bea, come here. What's the matter? Tell me. What's wrong?'

'Oh Jeffrey. I've had a terrible week. I think I might be going mad or maybe it's a midlife crisis. Apparently, Cara is having a desperate one and we're the same age.'

'What do you mean? You had a great week! You got top marks in your communications assessment. We celebrated with bubbly last night. Don't you remember?'

'I do. Yes, well that was the one good thing, I suppose. I just mean apart from that. Things were not so good for me, Jeffrey. Not so good at all.'

Ping! I threw my phone on the floor.

'Beatrice! You'll break it! What's gotten into you? I don't understand.'

I put my head in my hands. 'Neither do I, Jeffrey. Neither do I.'

'Maybe it's the cocktail. I made strong ones tonight, because I felt like it. Why don't you go to bed, sleep it off and we'll talk this through tomorrow. How does that sound?' He was rubbing my back now. He was sooooo nice. And comforting. I got up and wobbled a bit. It was abundantly clear to both of us that I simply needed to go to sleep right away. We hugged and I hobbled off towards the door.

'Beatrice', he gently called after me.

'Yes?' I turned around.

'Don't forget to take off your makeup,' he said.

'I'm not wearing makeup,' I answered. 'It's just BB cream.'

'Still...' he whispered. 'It's important to maintain good habits when it comes to skincare, and cleansing is one of the most crucial things you can do.'

I nodded, still downcast. 'Is it? Okay, Jeffery, I will. Goodnight now.'

✧ ✧ ✧

ROCKS GET WORN down and they build themselves

back up again. That's what they do. And that was just what I would have to do. I got up, showered and put some foundation, lipgloss and mascara on. That was all the makeup I could muster. Jeffrey complimented me and smiled when I walked into the kitchen. 'Such a natural beauty,' he said.

I wore my boyfriend jeans, because I wasn't really a skinny jeans kind of girl. I blow dried my hair straight and kicked my fringe to the side. I was making an effort ahead of the arrival of a fashion model to our home this morning. Jeffrey was out in his office setting up the makeup station and I was brewing coffee when the doorbell rang.

I answered the door and was presented with a quintessential picture of youth before me. It was the same girl as last time. The one with the short, straight, cute, shiny bob and skintight jeans. This time no blazer, just a Billie Eilish t-shirt tucked in. She was even prettier close up with no makeup on.

'Hi!' she blurted out with what I could only imagine was the exuberance of youth. Yes, she definitely wasn't a geography student. None of them seemed so enthusiastic and carefree. 'I'm looking for Jeffrey!' I could see why he liked working with her. 'He's doing my makeup!' So bright and bubbly, it was infectious.

'Yes, come in, come in. He's just setting up. I'm Beatrice, his wife.'

'Ah yes, he told me. You work in UCND? I'm

"studying" there.' She used finger quotation marks when she said that.

'Yes, Jeffrey told me. Marketing, isn't it?'

'Yes, I'm in my second year.'

Oh, she must be even younger than I thought. 'Do you like it?' I asked.

'No, I hate it. I love modelling, though. That's what I really want to do.'

'Oh well, that's good that you already know,' I offered.

Jeffrey came out. 'Ah Laverne! It's good to see you again!'

'You too! It's contouring today, right?'

'Yes,' he answered. We should get cracking. It takes a while and I want to leave enough time at the end for photos.'

They went into his office and I sat down at the kitchen table. I just needed a moment to take it all in. My husband in fashion. It was a new leap for the family and it was happening so fast. His old job was low-key and unglamorous. And now this! The kids came in asking who was at the door and that was all the time I had to process the impending changes that Jeffrey's new career might bring.

We went to the park later that afternoon and while it looked as though I was fully occupied pushing the girls on the swings and assisting Daniel on the climbing frames, thoughts of what I should do about Henry plagued me throughout. Should I tell Jeffrey? He'd been honest with me about his affair with Linda and I felt a tad guilty about accusing him of being unfaithful. I suppose all the secrecy, text messages and vacant expressions were due to him quietly pursuing his secret career dreams. He was probably waiting for an opportunity to tell me. Neither of us wanted it to happen the way it actually did, with me finding him alone in our room caked in makeup on a Monday afternoon.

I was proud of him all the same. He didn't just wish or dream from afar, he took action and was already halfway there as far as I could see. I was proud of myself too. I'd embraced a negative situation, given it 100% of my efforts and I think I was managing to turn it around. It all seemed to be working out so far. I was thriving in my course and fully confident that my commitment would serve me well. A better lecturer and more effective communicator it would make me.

That night, the children went to bed earlier than usual due to the active afternoon at the playground, affording myself and Jeffrey some much needed quality time together. He asked if he could do my makeup.

'But, Jeffrey, we're not going out or anything. I don't need my makeup done.'

'I need practice and isn't it better to practise on your face than mine?' He had a point there. I wasn't sure what to say. 'Please?' he pleaded. 'You can cleanse straight away afterwards. I have some nice samples you can use.'

This was a step too far. His pleading made me self-conscious and strangely insecure. I needed time to come to grips with this passion of his that I'd only just discovered. I needed to process his new aspirations, not to mind the meandering path our lives were currently taking.

I was also cognisant of the fact that he felt I wasn't being supportive, when it was abundantly clear how supportive he'd been to me with my recent endeavours in the university. I looked at him, really looked at him and could tell he desperately wanted this, so I succumbed and followed him into his office. He had designated shelving for the makeup and skincare products. Everything was so neat and tidy, ever the professional, I mused. He pulled out a high stool for me and moved a tall mirror on wheels in front of us.

'Beatrice, I'm going to cleanse first. Is that okay?' he said, earnestly.

'Yeah, sure, you don't have to tell me what you're doing. Just go ahead and do it.'

'Well, I want to get the experience of working with a client and I actually would introduce each step as I move along. Is that okay?' he asked.

'Oh, I see. Right, go ahead.' I let him, despite feeling a bit awkward.

'So, now your face is clean and free of makeup. I'm going to start by priming the skin with this G1 Beauty Lane Primer.'

'Jeffrey, you don't need to name the brands! I'm not buying from you. At least, I hope you're not trying to sell me anything?' I asked with a smile.

'Okay, it's just that I would if you were a real customer. I'd earn commission on my orders, but yeah, you're right. I'll just tell you what I'm doing.'

It was peaceful in his office and everything he did to my skin felt amazing and smelled exquisite. He was definitely using top-of-the-range products on me and the whole experience made me feel special.

'You've got great skin, Beatrice, so clear. You hardly need concealer, but I'll dab a little under the eye area anyway.'

'For my dark circles, you mean?'

'Oh yeah, sorry about that. I'm aware I've been passing comments on your skin. It's just that I'm noticing everything these days. Right, on we go. Minimum foundation. I'm using a powder foundation for this. Look, feel this. It's my favourite purchase so far! A kabuki brush!'

I felt it. 'Wow!' I acknowledged.

'Yeah, I know, sexy, isn't it?' He was so enthused. I'd never seen him like this telling me about an IT project. This definitely was his calling. I could tell because I could feel his passion. If I were a random customer, I'd buy any product he recommended to me. Women would listen to him. I knew there and then he was going to make a success of this. He proceeded to sweep the kabuki brush delicately over my face, paying particular attention to my cheeks, forehead, nose and chin. It felt delicious on my skin. We kept locking eyes and smiling. He knew I was enjoying the experience. And I knew he was too.

I liked it so much. I never usually spent time on my makeup. It was generally a quick slap of something on my face and an absent-minded rub in.

He stood back to appreciate what he'd done so far. 'Okay, great! Let's work on the eyes next and take it from there. Look at this colour palette, Beatrice, and tell me which ones you like.'

This was so exciting! I felt like a princess! I chose the sparkly bluey-silver shade and Jeffrey said, 'No, that's not good for you. Let's look lower on the palette. We need a warm, goldy shade to accentuate the blue of your eyes. Here! I found it!' I just let him pick whatever he thought was most suitable for me. Sure, what did I know? I hardly wore makeup, but I had a funny feeling that was going to change if my husband planned to become a professional makeup artist.

Eventually, he completed the look and was so

proud, he took numerous photos of me. We went into the living room to have a glass of wine before hitting the hay. We'd been planning to watch *Ozark*, but got chatting instead and forgot all about it. Out of the blue, Jeffrey gave me a compliment that I wasn't expecting. He was staring intently and I assumed he was still analysing his makeup artistry, but I was wrong. He was admiring me.

'Beatrice, you're so much prettier than all of the models I've worked on so far.' I shook with laughter. 'Jeffrey, what are you talking about? That girl today, Laverne, was a stunner and at least twenty years younger than me. Are you off your rocker?'

'No. No, I'm not. Granted, she is a very pretty girl, but look at you. Your face is so fresh and youthful and your beauty is classic and natural. I've always been attracted to your skin. It's so vibrant and abundantly clear.'

'It is? I mean, it is now, because you've worked your magic on it. But lately I've been so stressed and tired, I think I've aged ten years in about two weeks!'

'No, you still look to be in your early thirties. You did look tired when you arrived back from Glen Minogue, but I think the salty sea air may have dried out your skin, not to mention all the driving.'

'Yeah, and I didn't get much sleep that weekend either.'

'Oh, wasn't the hotel bed comfortable?'

I looked at him, my devoted, loving husband and super dad to our three children. He deserved honesty. He deserved the truth.

Chapter Sixteen

'JEFFREY, THERE'S SOMETHING I need to tell you about that weekend.'

'Oh, there's something I want to tell you too.'

'Is there?' Suddenly, I felt mightily insecure. Maybe my doubts had substance. Maybe there was something going on. Maybe I was right not to trust him completely, given he'd cheated before.

'Okay, you first,' I offered.

'No, no, you mentioned you wanted to say something first, so go ahead.'

'No, honestly, I insist. It wasn't important anyway. I'll tell you some other time. Yours sounded more vital. Mine was only something small and insignificant.'

He stared at me, into my eyes. 'Yes, mine was vitally important.' He reached out his hand and brushed my cheek. He leaned towards me. 'Beatrice, I've missed you so much. What's happened to us? To our marriage? To us as a couple?'

Oh my God, I wasn't expecting that. So heartfelt, so loving. He was right. We were an amazing couple, especially back when we first got together. We let it all go. The kids, our jobs, our busy household zapped our passion away and drove us apart. As did Jeffrey's affair, of course, but I didn't want to think about that now. I wanted to stare back into Jeffrey's deep, sultry brown eyes and get lost in them like I used to. So, I did. We both maintained eye contact and I grabbed his hand that was stroking my face. I kissed it and closed my eyes. He was right. What had happened to us? When I opened my eyes, he drew me close to him and we kissed each other like we did when we first dated. I ran my hand through his luscious, black hair and he groaned with pleasure. 'I always loved when you did that,' he whispered. So I did it again, massaging his scalp deeper, eliciting louder, more responsive sounds from him.

He pulled me onto his lap and I straddled him. He stood and lifted me. I clung on tight and he carried me to bed. We made love for the first time in a long time and somehow it seemed to make sense that we would do this. I still fancied him like crazy, even though I often doubted him and his love for me. But, tonight, he gave me no reason to doubt him any longer. I felt him return my passion with gusto. We hugged each other tight afterwards and laughed. We giggled at how stupid we'd been for leaving it so long. Jeffrey made it abundantly clear that we wouldn't and shouldn't neglect each other from now on, no matter what else was going on in our lives. Not our careers, our personal development, the kids, our families, nothing. We would put each other's needs at the fore and keep each other happy. I agreed and smiled and kissed him, until I got so tired, I just rolled over.

He turned off his bedside lamp and gently tapped me on the shoulder.

'Hmmm?' I said, with a post-coital smile still lingering on my lips.

'Beatrice, don't forget to take off your makeup. The sample cleansers are in the bathroom cabinet on the right.' Then he rolled over and I believe I heard him snore.

THERE WAS NO doubt our night together brought us closer. I had Jeffrey to thank for it. He was the one who instigated it and I'm so glad he did. The following weekend, when the kids went to bed early, we got frisky on the couch, until he reminded me of something.

'Hey, remember last week? You wanted to share something with me. You never did. What was it?'

'Oh, that. No, it's not important. Don't worry about it.'

'Of course it's important or you wouldn't have

mentioned it. C'mon, let's hear it.'

I pulled back. My heart started racing. I picked up the mojito he'd made for me and took a sip to settle my nerves.

'Well, I don't, Jeffrey. It sort of seemed important then, but not anymore. Can we just leave it?'

'Is everything okay?'

'Yeah, it is. I just need a minute, that's all.' My phone beeped. Twice in a row. At this hour on a Saturday night, there was only one person it could be.

'Go ahead. Check it,' Jeffrey said and he tucked his shirt back in. Then he picked up his drink and had a swig too.

I read my messages.

Henry
I take it you've fixed things up with Jeremy

Henry
If not, you know where I am x

Oh God, I should really reply to him sometime when I'm feeling measured and sober. I made a mental note.

'Well? Anything important?' Jeffrey enquired.

'Em, well, if you must know, it's Henry. I think I mentioned him to you before? My contact in the west.'

'Oh yeah, yeah you did. Why is he texting you

at this hour on a Saturday night? It's hardly rock business, is it?' He raised his eyebrows and had a smile in his eyes. I loved his eyes. They were vibrant, shiny and chocolate brown in colour. He was the only person I knew who could still look sexy when he was tired. He didn't get the dark under eye circles, like me. He just got this vacant, spaced out look that reminded me of a rockstar on drugs, especially when he ran his fingers through his hair and messed it up. Super sexy.

'No, no it's unrelated to the project. He sends me photos sometimes. You know, he's a fisherman, so he gets up and out on the boat at the crack of dawn. He knows I love the beach in Glan Mahogue, so he often shares a sunrise photo with me.' All true! Has happened. He did. Henry did. Fifty percent of the messages he sent last weekend were shots of the spectacular local scenery that he knew I'd appreciate.

'Really?' Jeffrey raised his brow questioningly. Oh no, did I say too much? Did I give the game away? Was Jeffrey suspicious? Of course, it did sound awfully romantic sharing sunrise scenes with a colleague. Shit! I'd have to tell him now. I'll have to reveal the details of my sordid, twisted rendezvous with Henry in his caravan. I looked at my hand with disgust. The lazy, limp one that dropped and fell on another man's you know what and turned it into wood. It was an accident, of course. I didn't mean to bring Henry to such great heights. I'd had a lot of wine. I thought my husband was cheating on me. I saw a young, attractive lady leaving OUR house that morning. What was I supposed to think? Anyone in my situation would have followed the same course of action after seeing that. It was a perfectly reasonable response to seeing one's husband cavorting with a strange woman on the doorstep of the family home. Perfectly reasonable.

Jeffrey frightened me when he interrupted my internal tirade.

'What?' I almost barked.

'Can I see?' he asked, sheepishly. *Oh no, he knows. He's onto me. He knows there's something going on that shouldn't be going on. He sees through me.* He has clocked my terror. Just when everything seemed to be falling into place—our marriage, my career, his chosen career path, my course, his course… 'Ahhhh!' He frightened me again.

'What's up with you tonight? Is the cocktail too strong for you? Here, let me get you some water. He came back with a pint glass and sat down beside me.

I wanted to get the phrasing right. Language was so important in these delicate circumstances. I knew that already, but was reminded of it in my communications course. I didn't want to blurt out something like, *'I let Henry fondle my breast and then my hand sort of accidentally fell down to his privates.'* No, I needed to consider the terminology. Breasts, yes that was okay. There was even a culinary, innocent ring to that word, conjuring up a Sunday roast chicken with the family perhaps, but let's see... Hmmm, how would I refer to Henry's genitalia in a similar nonchalant, harmless fashion?

I suppose I could just use the anatomically correct word for his organ. Penis. Yes, I'd just tell Jeffrey that I simply brushed off another man's penis and, rather by accident, he became erect. *Does that sound okay? Or should I say willy? Is it easier on the ears than penis?* I could say that my hand fell on Henry's willy, but it's okay because I only felt it through his jeans. And, to be fair, as we all know, denim is a fairly thick, sturdy material when you compare it to cotton or silk. So, I barely felt anything through it. How could I? Denim is like a sheet of armour, especially with the zip zipped up and no indelicate rips or openings.

Then I'd reassure Jeffrey that in actual fact, the whole fiasco was a big misunderstanding. A drink-fuelled one. An accidental rumble in his caravan. We had to sit close together. The lack of space dictated it. I mean, where were we supposed to fit our hands, if not under each other's clothes? Any two people squashed together on that ridiculous excuse for a couch would have done exactly the same thing. We were tragically limited, spacewise.

I sat back and rubbed my head. I was going to need painkillers before the night was out.

'So, show me then,' Jeffrey interrupted my thoughts again.

'Hmmm? Show you what?' I turned to him with guilt-ridden eyes.

'Beatrice, listen to me. There's this competition coming up. It's huge, I mean absolutely MASSIVE!' He looked at me, wide-eyed, like a lunatic.

'Jeffrey, what on earth are you talking about?' Why would he baffle me like this in my current mental state of crisis? My mind was already turning somersaults.

'Beatrice, listen. I've been researching this all week. There's an open competition coming up for amateur fashion photographers. I could make a name for myself with this one. Look here.' He reached for his phone and showed me an advertisement on Instagram. The only words I registered were LOCATION LOCATION LOCATION!!! It was something about a fashion shoot on location in Ireland. Jeffrey had ideas. He blurted out about ten, there and then on the couch. I ditched my water and resumed my cocktail. My head was sore. He was losing me. I just caught the tail end of what he was saying—

'And you keep telling me how beautiful and

remote Glen Minogue is, so I wondered if that could be my location. Let's have a look at those pictures Harry sent.'

Okay, he was interested in Glan Mahogue. Not in what I got up to while I was there. This was good. This was easing my developing headache. I scrolled through my phone and found a few scenic shots from Henry.

'Oh my God, Beatrice! It's coming! The vision is appearing in my head as we speak. I can see it. The boat, the beach, the sky, the cliffs!' he howled with delight. 'I've found it! That's the place!' He caught my shoulders and looked at me, intently, as if our lives depended on what he was about to say. 'Beatrice! You HAVE to take me there!!'

✧ ✧ ✧

I TRIED TO talk him out of it. I told him it wasn't actually that great and Galway would more likely be a better bet, or somewhere even farther south. I reminded him of the 'sunny southeast', but alas, he was having none of it. Henry's photos had sealed the deal for Jeffrey, as they contained the exact location for Jeffrey's 'money shot', as he called it. I was personally mortified at the thoughts of going back there. I mean, there would be absolutely no way of avoiding Henry if I found myself in Glan Mahogue again. Half the community knew who I was at this stage, as we had project-related questions for every Tom, Dick and Harry that lived there.

On the other hand, I was quite relieved that this new exciting adventure meant that I didn't have to go into detail trying to explain what happened with Henry's organ and my mammary glands in his pokey little caravan. I could postpone that story for another time. Or never. There were other things to consider now, like getting grand-parents to take the kids for the weekend, hiring a few models for the photoshoot and renting some expensive photography equipment to execute the all important 'money shot'.

Chapter Seventeen

OF COURSE, I had to inform Henry. I rang him to avoid extensive back and forth with text messages.

'You're coming to see me! I knew you'd come back, Beatrice! The beach here in Glan Mahogue is like a magnet. It pulls people back!'

'Yeah, it really is beautiful there, Henry.'

'And the wine in *The Shed*! No doubt you're coming back for more of that!'

'Well, actually, this is going to be a different kind of trip. You have to understand, I'm returning to help Jeffrey with a project. You know, Jeffrey, my husband?'

'So you say, Beatrice, so you say.'

'No, no, not 'so I say', he really IS my husband and I'll be returning with him, as his wife. We reconciled 100% and I want you to know this, because you'll probably meet him and I don't want you to have any expectations regarding me and you. Does that make sense, Henry?'

'Ah, there's always hope, Beatrice. Stranger

things have happened!'

'No, Henry, the very reason I made this phone call was to quash any hope you might be harbouring ahead of our visit. Do you understand what I'm trying to say?'

'So, you won't be staying the night in my caravan?'

'No, we've booked into the nearest hotel. The one I should have stayed in the last time.'

'Ah now, you slept soundly in my bed. I heard the snores to prove it!'

'Okay, Henry, about that night. Could we just keep it between us? No one else needs to know what went on, do they?'

'Keep schtum. You have my word.'

'Oh, thanks, Henry, that means so much to me. You've no idea.' I was genuinely grateful.

'Oh of course, I won't breathe a word. Otherwise, it may never happen again and we don't want that now, do we? It'll be our little secret, Beatrice, and I look forward to the next time!' He sounded chuffed with himself as he hung up. I put my head in my hands. Oh Lord, how did I get here? How had my life come to this? Everything that was important to me now hangs on the word of Henry McCormack. I felt like crying and would have if I had the time, but there was simply too much to do. I had to prepare notes for my Friday lectures, finish a written assignment for my communications course and pack three weekend bags for the kids for their 'holiday' in Granny and Grandad's.

Jeffrey was in the same boat, swamped with items to cross off his to-do list. He was busy hiring equipment and models and dictating to them what clothes they needed to bring for the shoot. From the snippets I overheard, gold bikinis were imperative. I shuddered. Wait until they felt the bitter Atlantic wind. I threw in a few blankets for the models to wrap themselves in between shots.

When the bags were packed, I sat down. Gold bikinis—my husband and the father of my three children, was asking women in their twenties to pack gold bikinis. Hmmmm. Was this still the man I married? I rubbed my forehead. Had my husband's metrosexuality escaped my attention all these years we'd been together? I mean, I always knew he was vain. He looked after himself. He worked out, moisturised and went for more haircuts than me. He was always interested in fashion too. He shopped for clothes regularly, more so than most men I'd assume. I always blindly accepted all of those things. Yes, I knew he cared about his appearance. I just didn't know he cared about mine.

The comments on my skin of late, the subtle nudges towards double cleansing, the arrival of free samples in the bathroom cabinet—all of this was slowly being revealed to me. He cared about my outward appearance. This was a new added pressure for me. As if there weren't enough. Jeffrey seemed like he was scrutinising my appearance in efforts to learn more about anti-aging products for women. I was his guinea pig.

But all this scrutiny—it was too much. What would happen when my lines got deeper, my hair grew greyer and those crows feet around my eyes spread out? What would happen then? Would he want to replace me with someone ten years younger? And now, he was working with models twenty years younger. Would he get tempted by them? I bet a fair few would develop a crush on him. *Oh damn you, Jeffrey! Why does your dream career have to be so glamorous? Why does it have to be so far removed from my comfort zone?*

Then I realised I was being selfish. My comfort zone was geography. Rocks and rugged landscapes were my passion. Jeffrey supported me in the pursuit of my dreams. Now it was my turn to be supportive. He needed me. I vowed to rise to the challenge. These pep talks in my mind always provided clarity. I wondered if other people engaged in this kind of self-talk. Maybe I'd promote it to my students one day. After the communications course, I think I could sell anything!

✧ ✧ ✧

THE KIDS WERE thrilled to be going on 'holidays'! Granny and Grandad were only delighted to be spending the weekend with their beloved grandkids. I managed to wrangle Friday afternoon off by providing course material for my students to study. Jeffrey got his IT work finished in three days this week rather than the usual four, so he had the car packed, everything booked, kids dropped off and we were ready to hit the road to Glan Mahogue by two pm.

The three models he'd booked were due to get the train together and Jeffrey would pick them up from the train station, but just as we were pulling out of the driveway, he got a call from Laverne. She'd missed the train. He cleared a seat in the back and we swung by her place to collect her. A pack of cigarettes fell out of her jacket pocket as they were loading in her stuff. Jeffrey freaked out and berated her for smoking. He rattled off a five-minute speech about the internal damage she was doing to her lungs, not to mention the external repercussions for her skin. I checked my watch. We were on a tight schedule. I broke Jeffrey's rant to tell him we needed to get a move on. We would have to drop our things at the hotel to make space in the car for the other two models on the train. They surely wouldn't be happy to be left waiting at the station.

With that, we set off in earnest. Jeffrey driving, me navigating and Laverne sulking in the backseat, because the driver refused to stop the car for a smoke break. I tried to dissipate the tension by pressing play on my Guns N' Roses CD, but Jeffrey immediately replaced it with the latest Dua Lipa. That modern pop meant nothing to forty-year-old me, but seemed to put a smile on both Jeffrey and Laverne's faces.

I shook my head. My husband, I thought, down with the kids. Fashion photographer. Makeup artist. Hiring models in gold bikinis. I threw my head back. Life was moving at such great speed. How could I keep up? Could I keep up? I took a deep breath. Time would tell.

✧ ✧ ✧

THE JOURNEY WENT smoothly in the end, especially when Jeffrey needed to stop for petrol and I told Laverne to sneak off for a cigarette. She had plenty of gum and we rolled down the windows so he wouldn't get the whiff. He dropped us at the hotel, outside town, and went to collect the other two models.

The three of them were sharing a triple room with all expenses paid by Jeffrey, and we had our own room. This was the hotel that the admin was going to book for me, had I not trusted Henry with my arrangements. My first trip to Glan Mahogue would have been so different if I'd just stayed here. More productive and focussed, I imagined. Henry's little caravan was most distracting. Still, at least I managed to complete the work outlined for Stage 1 of the project.

We all had an early night and arranged to meet for breakfast at eight am. Myself and Jeffrey made love straight away when we got into bed. I think it was the excitement of being away together in a fresh hotel room. It was all coming back to us—The limerence we felt when we first got together. It was still there. It continued to exist after all these years. I banished thoughts of whether it would endure with the passing of time. I didn't want to entertain that prospect.

Jeffrey wanted to make it to his location on the beach as early as possible to get set up. Then we would just have to wait until the sun was at the right angle to capture the photo.

I braced myself, because I knew as soon as we got to the beach we would meet Henry. He'd probably be returning from his early morning fishing excursion. My stomach was tied up in knots. I just really hoped he wouldn't put his foot in it. I had serious doubts about whether I could trust him to be discreet. I didn't have much time to dwell on it as I was Jeffrey's right-hand man for this venture. I was loading and carrying equipment, while sharing the schedule with the models. It was bustling and hectic, but kind of exciting too.

Sure enough, Henry was walking along the beach on his way back to his caravan. I spotted his brand new pearly whites twinkling in the distance. He was beaming ear to ear. I gave Jeffrey a heads up that this was the local fisherman I'd been paired with for the project. As we got closer, Jeffrey held out his hand and exclaimed, 'Harry! A pleasure to meet you!'

Henry only had eyes for me. 'Beatrice! You're back! I knew you'd come back!'

'Henry, it's good to see you again. This is my husband, Jeffrey,' I replied.

Then, Jeffrey said, 'Harry?' and Henry nodded and said, 'Jeremy,' and they both shook hands. I took a breath. Okay, I thought, the initial introductions were over. We could move on. I proceeded to introduce Henry to Laverne, Christine and Maya, as soon as they caught up with us. His face lit up as he announced Glan Mahogue had never witnessed such glamour. The girls were very taken with him, worryingly so, I decided.

Henry continued on to his caravan to refrigerate the fish he'd caught and said he'd come back to help us get set up. His knowledge about the movement of the sun and the timing of it would, no doubt, prove invaluable to Jeffrey, who was all about getting the lighting just right.

As soon as he arrived back with ice-pops for everyone, the flirting began. He wasn't giving up on me, despite the presence of my husband, but he was relentless with the three models, who were rising to his bait. Laverne let it slip that she would be turning twenty the following week and with that, Henry announced a party back in his caravan as soon as the photo session ended. Myself and Jeffrey immediately made excuses that we wouldn't be able to attend, because we'd have lots of work to do following the shoot. As Jeffrey put it, the bulk of the work would have to be done post shoot to edit the photo according to the competition's guidelines. Henry wasn't accepting it.

'Ah Beatrice, I have your favourite white wine in a bucket of ice chilling for you. You'll come for a while. Jeremy can get down to business back at the hotel. You stay with me and the girls and I'll invite a few of the locals to join us. We might take the party to *The Shed* afterwards and who knows, maybe we'll all end up in *The Bed* together!'

Jeffrey looked up with a horrified expression. 'Don't worry,' I whispered, 'I'll explain later.' The three girls wanted to hear all about the local hangouts that Henry mentioned and he had them exploding with laughter for half the afternoon. It was up to me and Jeffrey to get the serious prep done. We broke for lunch, leaving the equipment covered on the beach to protect it from sand. Luckily, it was a clear day with no rain forecasted. Henry promised to keep an eye on everything, while we returned to the hotel for a quick bite.

With Henry's analysis in mind, Jeffrey deemed the ideal photo opportunity time to be approximately 6.30pm, when the sky would be starting to change colour. He wanted us to be ready to shoot any time from 5.20 though, just in case an interesting glimmer appeared. We were ordered back to the beach with costumes in tow, after lunch. The three girls wore their gold bikinis under their attire on glowing, prepped, tanned skin. Their hair was down because Jeffrey wanted it to blow naturally in the wind. They had done their own makeup that morning, but Jeffrey insisted on a touch up to coordinate with the colours on the beach, pre photo shoot. He also brought along some body glitter shimmer and I wondered if he was planning to apply that himself. I was fully certain Henry would offer to help if that was the case.

I seemed to accidentally develop a bond with Laverne, where she relied on me to facilitate her secret smoke breaks. She'd give me a nod and I'd find a substantial rock for her to hide behind, so that Jeffrey wouldn't clock she was smoking. He was effectively her boss for the weekend and she didn't want to make him angry. I was aiding and abetting her unhealthy habit, so I'd also be in the firing line if Jeffrey happened to discover the 'smoking rock'. It was fun for me to find interesting slabs for her. I imparted some geological details about the rocks I'd chosen, but unfortunately she showed no interest. The sad thing was, she reminded me of my geography students. They showed a similar lack of interest in rock formation. Always a source of disappointment for me, as a long-time lover of rock. I tried not to let it get to me. After all, this field trip was about fashion and glamour, not beach rock and seaweed.

✧ ✧ ✧

WE REHEARSED ALL afternoon for the shoot, but Jeffrey wasn't satisfied. 'I need them farther back, closer to the sea', he yelled, but everytime they moved back, they got splashed by the waves and screamed. The Atlantic ocean was icy cold. And then, lo and behold, Henry had an idea!

'I'll take them out on my boat. Just a tad. At least they'll be dry in it. The waves won't splash them, because we'll be riding the waves.' I noticed he locked eyes with Laverne when he mentioned 'riding the waves'. Oooh, I despaired, she was only nineteen years old!

Jeffrey liked the idea, but not the 'riding the waves' part. He only wanted the boat to be used as protection against the splashing water. There was enough space in the boat for all the elements he had envisaged. Henry suggested he should get in the boat with the models to steady it, if nothing else. The hope in his eyes was obvious.

Surprisingly, Jeffrey acknowledged his request and toyed with the idea of hiding Henry or getting him to duck for the shot, but also didn't want the boat to capsize or the girls to feel unsafe. Jeffrey whispered to me that Henry had appropriate coloured eyes for an ocean shot. I agreed, and he went on to compliment his white teeth and cheeky grin. He also thought his thick, wavy hair would look great in the shot with the models, but was most disparaging of his attire. 'I'm not including him in the photo with that torn, raggy t-shirt on him. Beatrice, can you ask him discreetly if he has any better clothes?' I was mortified at the prospect of asking Henry to take off his clothes, but did as requested regardless. I could see Jeffrey was getting stressed.

I approached Henry.

Chapter Eighteen

'HEY HENRY, JEFFREY thinks you'd look great in the photo shoot with the models. How do you feel about going on camera?' I asked.

'With them? All three of them? Fantastic!'

'Okay, right, I thought so. Do you have any clean clothes back in your caravan?'

'What? What's wrong with this? This is from the nineties. You like nineties music, don't you?' He looked offended.

'Yes, indeed. That was my era. Well, that and the eighties. Look, em, there's nothing wrong with your t-shirt as such. It's just that it looks very worn. Have you got anything a bit fresher back in the caravan?'

He laughed leeringly. 'Are you just trying to get me back to the caravan to take my clothes off, Beatrice? That wine would be nicely cooled for you by now.'

'No, absolutely not. You do know that Jeremy is my husband, don't you?' I implored, while he stared back at me, blankly. 'I mean Jeffrey! Jeffrey is my husband and we're back together. You understand, don't you?' I was pleading at this stage.

'He was your husband the last time too and that didn't stop you,' Henry responded.

Shit, that was true. 'Henry, please, let's not get into this now. Look, do you have anything you could change into?'

'Well, I bought a new white t-shirt when I heard you were coming back to see me.'

'Perfect! That would be perfect!'

'And some pink, stripey boxers. I thought you might like them too, for the craic, y'know?'

'Em, no, no, just the t-shirt. Quick! Run, get the t-shirt and come back. This shot won't happen without you.'

I gave Jeffrey a thumbs up and he proceeded to apply eye pencil, lip pencil, blusher and bronzer to accentuate the girls' already highly defined features. He kept saying, 'you can't be too careful in this light.' Then, it was time for them to undress down to their skimpy bikinis and get this body shimmer thingy with sparkles in it rubbed all over their bodies. Jeffrey looked at me.

'Beatrice, help us out.' And, he threw a can to me. He applied it to Laverne, who screamed at how cold it was and I had to do Christine's and Maya's. We all burst into giggles at all the yelping and then turned when we heard Henry shout,

'Guys! Wait for me!'

We were taken aback at the vision of him in the crisp, white t-shirt running along the beach. He looked like a movie star. The clean, white colour brought out the tan in his lean, muscular arms. It also accentuated the blue of his eyes and we all seemed to say in unison something like, 'oh wow, Henry, you look great!' He was beaming ear to ear and laid out his arms for some body glitter too. Laverne grabbed the can and obliged. *She's only nineteen!* I screamed (in my head).

Then, it was time. Jeffrey placed everyone in his desired position on the boat. He did some chopping and changing amid their squeals and giggles, as the boat rocked from side to side. It ended up with Henry in the middle, sitting down and the three girls around him with their hands on his shoulders. There were butts sticking out and ample cleavage on show, due to the way they were bending down.

'Really, Jeffrey? Isn't that a bit racy? I mean, I thought the scenic background was more important, but believe me, if you leave them like that, no one will even notice the sun setting in the sky behind.'

'I know what I'm doing, Beatrice. Sex sells, even in the west of Ireland. They just need to float out a little and that'll be my shot.'

I stood back. He didn't seem to need my input.

He was the creative one and he knew exactly what he wanted. In the end, it was most unglamorous and uncomfortable for everyone involved, especially because Jeffrey had to take about one hundred shots to satisfy the perfectionist in him. The girls were getting very cold. Christine was seasick on the rocking boat and Maya was becoming impatient with Jeffrey's constant tweaks. Henry was the only one who seemed to thoroughly enjoy the whole experience. Honestly, the smile never left his face!

As soon as Jeffrey was satisfied, I ran out to the girls with blankets, afraid they may catch pneumonia on our watch. Henry offered to make them all hot whiskeys and got on his phone for the next half hour inviting disbelieving locals to his caravan containing three Dublin models. In the end, he had to take photos of them for his mates to prove they were real. It was mainly myself and Jeffrey who cleaned up. The girls were shivery in their blankets and kept busy posing and pouting for Henry photos. We declined the offer of the caravan booze-up and Henry promised he'd arrange for the girls to get a taxi back to the hotel later that night. I really hoped I could trust him but was too tired to argue.

Jeffrey grabbed my hand and squeezed it on the way to the car. He made it abundantly clear that he was glad it was just the two of us returning to the hotel. Just the two of us.

✧ ✧ ✧

HE STAYED UP until midnight editing the photo to comply with competition requirements. He was chuffed with the end result and promptly named it 'Glan Miami', due to the wild Irish landscape combined with glamorous beach babes on board the boat. There was massive sex appeal in it with their provocative twerking poses and Henry looked like Ireland's next top model perched in the middle of all the pizzazz. He added an earthy ruggedness to the high-end glitz and commanded much attention with his pearly whites flashing mid screen. The white of his t-shirt accentuated his fisherman's suntan and he seemed to have a natural glow. The allure of his facial expression was remarkable and even Jeffrey couldn't deny his appeal.

'The addition of this guy in the photo might just win the competition for me. He really draws you in, doesn't he? I can see why you kept in touch with him, Beatrice.'

I didn't know what to say, so I nodded and smiled. As it turned out, I had no choice BUT to keep in touch with Henry. He demanded it, and in fairness, it had paid off. As Jeffrey admitted, the photo was a million times more attractive with the presence of Henry.

Jeffrey was so psyched on completion of the process that we had the most intense sex of our lives with each other well into the early hours. We slept through breakfast the next morning and had a slow, sensual, lazy, childless start to the day, just like real lovers.

✧ ✧ ✧

THERE WAS NO sign of the three girls when Jeffrey was settling the bill at reception. I volunteered to go to their room and hurry them along. We were supposed to drop them to the train station at 12 pm for their return journey. I found them slumped in their beds with aching heads and noticed golden glitter all over the crisp white bed sheets. Laverne seemed to be the only one able to answer my questions. It sounded like *The Bed* served alcohol until four am and they only got back to the hotel around five. They were all in bits. I vowed to kill Henry the next time I saw him. I had to help each of them get dressed and pack up. Suddenly, it didn't feel like a weekend away without the kids. I was in full Mammy mode getting these three young ladies on the train back to Dublin.

Their phones kept buzzing in the car all the way to the train station. Henry had them in hysterics. He was texting each of them to ask when they'd be coming back to Glan Mahogue to see him. I smiled too, mainly because I realised the pressure would be off me. He seemed to have a new, younger love interest now. Or two. Or three.

✧ ✧ ✧

THANK GOODNESS A bit of normality ensued in the following weeks. Jeffrey threw himself into the fashion photography course and I was so enraptured in my communications course that we hardly saw each other. The grandparents helped out with minding the children to allow us progress with our respective extra-curricular endeavours.

I was smashing the communications course. The facilitator was lavishing praise upon me and asking me to model communicative techniques for the class. I was sure I'd be getting top marks when it came to my appraisal and assessment.

I no longer received text messages from Henry. According to Jeffrey, one of the models, Christine, was still in touch with him and planning to get the train to visit him soon. I was relieved. Christine was twenty-five and much more mature than young Laverne. She would let Henry know what's what. I had no doubt.

IT WAS DURING the summer break that the results of the fashion shoot competition were due to be announced. Jeffrey initially made the longlist and then the shortlist, so he was full of high hopes. I was only beginning to realise what he meant when he told me all those weeks ago that 'this could be big'. It was a VIP affair, with celebrity MCs from our national broadcasting TV station, RTE1. The winner would get a centre page spread in Ireland's version of *Vanity Fair* and a feature on the nation's most popular TV fashion show, *County Catwalk*. He was right. This was massive and I had no doubt that the competition winner would become an overnight celebrity sensation in Ireland. The hype surrounding the competition had already started, with regular advertisements on *County Catwalk* and social media.

We were invited to attend the ceremony in the studios of RTE, where they would announce the winner and runner-up, both of whom would win a substantial amount of prize money, together with opportunities to work with the best in the business.

I had no idea what to wear. Jeffrey not only bought me a dress and suitable high-heeled shoes, but also offered to do my makeup for the event. The only thing I had to do was shower and get a blowdry.

On the night, Jeffrey wore a crisp, white shirt, long skinny black tie and an immaculately fitted black suit. His early hours in our home gym paid off and he looked buff. Unfortunately, he was a nervous wreck, though. I guess it meant so much to him and if he won, it would be a huge opportunity to make a name for himself. As soon as my makeup was done, I left him to his own devices, not wanting to fuss him further. It was a silent taxi ride. I think he may have been meditating. Again, I didn't bother him too much, only to admire him and tell him he looked great.

I looked great too. He'd done an amazing job with my makeup, sticking to the natural look that I favoured. We scrubbed up well as a very glamorous couple and fit right in with all the celebrity faces knocking about. We were photographed on our way in and then Jeffrey was whisked away from me for interviews with the other finalists. I didn't see him again until we took our seats ahead of the big announcement. I'd kept myself busy with prosecco, hors d'oeuvres and people watching. I didn't mind being left alone.

The first runner-up photo was named as 'Mingle in Dingle' and the very shy, overwhelmed photographer from Co Kerry gave a thank you speech. The next announcement was the big one. Jeffrey wasn't interested in being a runner up. He wanted gold.

'And, the winner is...'Glan Miami' by Jeffrey Walsh!' I felt him freeze and then melt. He turned to me, kissed me quickly on the lips and went to accept his award on the stage. A brief interview followed and everyone wanted a piece of him. They not only wanted to know all about the fashion shoot and location, but also where he'd bought his suit and shoes, and even what moisturiser he was wearing. I was thrilled for him and popped outside to ring the grandparents to share the good news. Lauren was still up and sounded ecstatic as she screamed, 'Daddy won! Daddy won!'

Jeffrey approached me when I returned inside and handed me a glass of champagne.

'I was looking for you', he said.

'I rang the folks to share the fab news. Lauren was jumping on the bed with excitement!' We laughed.

'Hey, I need to go and mingle. There's some seriously important names here that I simply must make contact with. Will you be okay on your own, or do you want to come with me?'

That was a loaded question. I knew I'd only be trailing after him like a needy puppy. There was already a queue forming around us, each person with a different logo on their microphone. It was a combination of radio stations, TV and magazine groups. I imagined none of them wanted to discuss rock formations or climate change with me, so I thought it better to leave him to it. I was about to kiss him goodbye, when a tall, spindly fashionista grabbed his arm and demanded, 'Jeffrey, darling, over here!' They were an excited, pushy bunch and I decided it wasn't my scene. I finished my glass of champagne, not wanting to waste the good stuff and texted Jeffrey that I was leaving.

He didn't reply. I guess he didn't have time.

Chapter Nineteen

IT SEEMED AS though Jeffrey's phone never stopped beeping following the all-important win. He reduced his hours to part time in his current IT project in order to devote time to his newfound career. From what I could gather, he was in demand with requests from TV, radio, magazines, newspapers and social media platforms. It was hectic, but brilliant for him. I thought everything was going his way, just as he planned, yet he didn't seem fulfilled. Over dinner, he rubbed his forehead and pinched the bridge of his nose as if to offset a headache. He complained of feeling stressed and tired, which was something he'd never done up to now. Was it a case of 'be careful what you wish for'?

I tried to facilitate his new career choice and busy lifestyle by being around more often for the kids. I cooked for them, but unlike Jeffrey, I followed cookbook recipes to a T. I was afraid that if I was too creative or adventurous, no one would eat it. I had a few successes, mainly thanks to

Donal Skehan.

On the rare occasion when I had a moment to think, I observed the distance increasing between me and Jeffrey. This was mainly due to his new work commitments, many of which involved late nights or long, boozy evenings. I didn't feel comfortable with these changes. I lay awake at night waiting to hear his keys in the door. Only then would I nod off. He seemed not to be enjoying his success to the fullest, and tired too, as he wasn't used to such a lack of routine.

In the meantime, I received my results from the exams and practicals I'd done as part of the communications course. I was over the moon to receive top grades and even a job offer to become a part-time facilitator. My good news was met with a measured response from family and friends compared to the fanfare that Jeffrey got for his big win. I didn't mind, though. It meant the world to me and I knew it would improve my relationship with my students forever more. I no longer craved vindication for my personal achievements. I knew what I wanted for myself career-wise and I was well on my way. In contrast to Jeffrey, I felt elated by my success in the communications course and planned to use every single communicative technique I'd learned in my lectures henceforth.

My own private sense of satisfaction that I was smashing my career goals made me question why

Jeffrey sacrificed so much to persevere with a career that clearly brought him little joy. Was it that he simply wasn't cut out for it? Was forty too old to change tack? I couldn't figure it out but resolved to get to the bottom of it before returning to uni.

In early September, there was one adventure that I agreed to share with Jeffrey. The fashion TV show *County Catwalk* wanted to dedicate an episode to Jeffrey on location. They wished to go to Glan Mahogue, use the same models, but get a few alternative shots around the remote area, now known as 'Glan Miami'. I thought one last trip before I returned to the grind would do me good—for nostalgia's sake, if nothing else.

I mainly went along to enjoy the scenery and collect some rocks from the beach. I kept a stash in the corner of our back garden at home, unsure of what I would eventually do with them. As we approached the little town of Glan Mahogue, I got a whiff of the sea air and instantly felt glad I came.

We stayed in the same hotel as last time, but didn't make love like we did on those two nights together. Jeffrey was a bit nervous about recreating the shoot the following day and about what he would say on the live VT. I didn't mind too much. I'd brought along the latest edition of *National Geographic*, so that kept me more than occupied. It almost seemed as though Jeffrey had forgotten that this was a special hotel for us, rekindling our dormant romance just a few months ago. Or, that said, if he hadn't forgotten and did remember its significance, it was abundantly clear that it just didn't mean that much to him.

✧ ✧ ✧

I MET HENRY on the beach the next morning.

'Ah Beatrice, great to see you back here in Glan Mahogue!'

'Or Glan Miami, as we now know it!' I smiled. 'Are you something of a local celebrity now after the winning picture went viral?'

'Well, to tell you the truth, there's a few ladies travelling from Galway and Sligo and even as far away as Limerick asking for my whereabouts in *The Shed*. I've had to do a few guided tours of the beach and local area to show them around.'

'I bet you enjoyed that!' We both laughed. And then he turned serious. 'Did the models come along? The same ones as last time?'

'We couldn't get Laverne this time. She's back in uni, but Christine and Maya are here. They're meeting us shortly.'

He looked relieved when I mentioned Christine was coming back.

'I see you're wearing the same white t-shirt as last time?'

'If it ain't broke.' He winked. Then Jeffrey came along.

'We better get moving, guys. We've a lot to do today. I need your input on the aspect of the sun for the afternoon.'

'Well, Jeremy, a great win for us all. Thanks for the cheque you sent.'

'Of course, of course. It was a team effort and well deserved. Are you ready to go global now?' he asked.

'If it means another cheque in the post, I am! I might be able to build myself a house at this rate, if the money keeps rolling in,' Henry answered.

'You don't live in that caravan all year round, do you?' Jeffrey expressed some concern.

'Ah no, I move in with my parents for the winter months. Ah look, here come the girls!' Then he walked towards the ladies to welcome them back. He was in his element. Myself and Jeffrey locked eyes and chuckled. I didn't see much of him for the rest of the day as he was pulled aside for pieces to camera or to touch up makeup, or decide on costumes. I could tell already, this was going to be another big deal if it went as intended. I was happy for him that he was pursuing his passion for fashion. Happier for him than he seemed to be himself. He was flustered and stressed looking, but I suppose he simply wanted everything to be perfect.

It gave me a chance to go paddling, collect some shells and stroke some rocks. It was peaceful and therapeutic and I loved it. I loved Glan Mahogue, but feared this newfound fame and title of 'Glan Miami' would spoil it going forward. Now the general public knew about it and wanted to visit. They saw the VTs, read the magazine articles and listened to the radio interviews. They wanted to come and admire its splendour for themselves. The younger folk saw the beautiful models in skimpy bikinis and wanted to visit *The Shed* and *The Bed*. Some wanted selfies with Henry, Glan Mahogue's most famous bachelor! His caravan was becoming a landmark and I'd seen the hilarious signposts—'This way for Henry's Caravan'.

I knew it was beneficial for the locals to have their town on the map and bring life to it. *The Bed* and *The Shed* were already renovating and extending to include a restaurant, called *Get Fed*. I noticed flower pots on windowsills, walls getting painted and potholes getting filled. The locals went out of their way to be friendly to me, because they knew I was Jeffrey's wife and they were delighted with the fame and good fortune his competition win had afforded them. So, I guess it was a good thing overall, especially if it made the locals happy.

Henry finally consolidated his relationship with Christine and she spent the night with him in his caravan. I hung out with Maya the following day, because we were both at a loose end. We even travelled back ahead of the others, as Jeffrey wanted to do a photo shoot with Henry and Christine in his caravan. I raised my eyes. The world was going to know about Henry McCormack very soon. I could see huge life changes coming his way.

✧ ✧ ✧

SHORTLY AFTER WE returned from our trip out west, some sort of routine resumed. Jeffrey tried to avoid the late-night soirees and got back to being available for the school run at least. I was impressing both myself and Mr. Keel with my newly learned lecturing techniques. He was so thrilled with the turnaround in my delivery that he asked me to mentor some of the junior members of staff and teach them a few techniques I'd acquired at the course. I didn't really have time for any extra responsibilities, but for Mr. Keel, I'd push the boat out and oblige. I was extremely fond of him.

Even without the late nights, Jeffrey was still distant and seemed to be under pressure. I tried to talk to him about it, but he reassured me it was just difficult for him to deal with the speed of his new career and keep up with all the demands. He spent a lot of time in his office on calls and video calls, so the 'Do Not Disturb' sign was constantly visible. He hardly ever took it down anymore, which meant the kids and I barely entered his office, only to knock on the door and alert him that dinner was ready.

It actually got me reminiscing about our stint in couple's therapy, mainly because we were forced to communicate with each other back then. There was no avoiding it in a small, cosy room with a therapist. No one could get away with a 'Do Not Disturb' sign. I considered this option once again, if Jeffrey continued to resist my gentle requests for communication. I knew there was something wrong, something he wasn't telling me and it seemed out of character for him to turn away so often.

✧ ✧ ✧

A FEW DAYS later, I was washing the kids' tracksuits, when I realised Jeffrey's gym gear hadn't been washed in ages. I didn't know if maybe he just didn't have time to work out anymore or whether the laundry was accumulating and he didn't get an opportunity to throw a wash on. He was out at a makeup consultation, so I let myself into his office to look for the wash basket in the mini gym next door.

As I walked through his office, I smelled the

gorgeous lavender scented sticks. It smelled so fresh and clean, just like Jeffrey. I looked around and smiled, but got a fright when a notification beeped on his computer screen. I wondered if it was anything I needed to alert him of, so went over to check if I'd recognise the name. I almost fell to the floor when I discovered who it was.

IT WAS HER! I looked away and back again to recheck. Yes, definitely her. It was Dr. Linda, his former GP. The one he'd had the affair with. Why were they still in touch? Why was she messaging him? And why did she look so flawless and vibrant in her profile picture attached to her email account? It made me sick. I began to wonder if she could be the reason Jeffrey had been so distracted of late? Were they back together? Was this why he was showing absolutely zero interest in me since becoming famous? I wasn't young enough. Not attractive enough. I looked towards her photo again. *I'm not her. I'm not Linda.*

Maybe he'd never forgotten her. Why else would he be in contact with her now? You don't stay friends with someone you've had a steamy, passionate extramarital affair with, do you? I know I'd remained friendly with Henry, but that was different. We didn't have a sexy affair, but rather an accidental kiss that went on a few more seconds than it should have. It was so short and insignificant that neither of us felt much remorse afterwards. I mean, I didn't mean to make him erect and he probably didn't mean to kiss me. Our faces just fell into each other's out of awkwardness. Drunken awkwardness. Saying goodnight to someone you've just shared your greatest fears with on the tiniest two-seater ever invented was a difficult task. How could we have avoided getting intimate? There was no space for it NOT to happen!

But now I see I've nothing to feel guilty about. It actually makes perfect sense. Linda must have seen him on TV and contacted him. That relit their spark and that's why Jeffrey has completely gone off me. He's been so standoffish of late, so distant and jumpy. Well, it must be stressful trying to hide an extramarital affair from your wife that you've literally just gotten back together with. I put my hand to my head and cried. I couldn't believe I'd have to relive all of this. Oh God, not now. Not again. I massaged my forehead and tried to remember what I was doing in Jeffrey's office in the first place. Oh yeah, laundry. I went into the little gym next door. So, he was still working out. The basket was full, overflowing even. Of course he was working out. He had to try to impress Linda who was ten years his junior. He had to maintain his toned, defined physique to keep her interested. He definitely wasn't doing it for me, anyway. Never was. I never cared about his muscle tone and he knew it, but continued to hone it anyway.

I went over and kicked the basket to the floor. It was already close to falling anyway, with being so full. Then, I left his filthy, fresh-smelling office and turned on the washing machine with a half load.

Chapter Twenty

WHAT WAS I going to do? We had tried to make this marriage work. We'd gone to counselling and given it our all, only to find ourselves back at square one. I really thought this time had seemed different. I thought we were out of the woods, but I suppose once a cheater, always a cheater. I cried again into my hands as I turned on more cartoons for the kids. Under sixes were extremely unobservant and couldn't comprehend that their mother could cry just like them when she was sad. They saw me looking at them and Mia asked if I was chopping onions.

'Yes, yes that's it,' I lied. I just didn't know what to do. I felt so sorry for them that their devoted father was actually a double-crossing, lying, cheating shleeveen at the back of it all. They didn't deserve this. I didn't deserve this. I went into the kitchen to hatch a plan. I needed to get away. Away from the house and away from Jeffrey, so I could think clearly and really figure things out. My midterm break was coming up shortly. Maybe I'd book something for me and the kids. I wanted them with me whatever happened. We would stick together and Jeffrey could go and jump, for all I cared.

He came home that evening talking and laughing on the phone. He put his finger up when he saw me in the kitchen, as if to say, 'this is really important', and went into his office. He certainly made his priorities abundantly clear. I'd made some spaghetti bolognese and I turned the TV towards the dinner table. This evening we'd be watching *Madagascar* during dinner time. Anything to avoid a superficial conversation with Jeffrey. Anything.

✧ ✧ ✧

I MADE UP my mind. I was taking the kids with me. Just for a week. I needed to get away and I needed to think. It didn't take me long to figure out where I'd go. Glan Mahogue's rocky shores appeared to me in my dreams. I swallowed my pride and rang Henry.

'I insist,' he said. 'You can have my brother's cottage. It's at the other end of the beach. He'll be away that week with his girlfriend in Spain. He gives me full use of it whenever he's away, but I don't need it this time. Not with this Indian summer we're having. I'll be grand in my caravan.

The finest, in fact.'

'Oh Henry, you're a godsend. Thank you. And look, as I said, I need some headspace. I need to get away from Jeffrey for the week, so if he rings, don't tell him where I am. Got it?'

I had the kids' stuff packed the day before and put it all in my boot when no one was around. Jeffrey knew nothing of our impending departure. Neither did the kids, but I knew they'd be delighted to be going to a faraway beach, 'on the other side of the world'. They'd buy into my little adventure with them. I knew by this time next week I'd have my mind made up about my marriage, whether to stay or go. I was too muddled up at present to decide. I brought plenty of notepaper to make lists—pros and cons, that kind of thing.

When the time came to go, I left a note on the kitchen table for Jeffrey.

Jeffrey, I need some time to think about our marriage. It's clear to me you are not to be trusted. I'm taking the kids. We'll be fine. We'll be home next Saturday. Carry on as normal and don't worry about us. No contact, please. I really need this time to think. Don't mention this to the folks. They might worry.

Beatrice.

I woke the children extra early that morning on purpose, so desperate was I that they should sleep on the long journey. I was right. Within forty-five minutes, all three conked out. It was a peaceful journey. Jeffrey didn't hear us leaving. He was working out in his gym with loud music on. He usually did that for at least an hour on weekend mornings, and then by the time he showered, I predicted we'd be halfway there before he'd see the note on the table.

This time I knew exactly where I was going, so I didn't need to rely on Google maps. Any stress I'd felt whittled away when I saw the little sign-posts for Glan Mahogue. I just couldn't wait to show the kids the stony beach and splash about in the waves. I'd packed their wetsuits, just in case. Mia must have heard my excited squeals and she was the first to wake up.

'Mammy, Mammy, are we there yet? Are we there yet?' she demanded. That was when the others woke up too, both absolutely dying to go to the toilet. I was so glad we were only minutes away. We just about made it. Daniel did a wee against the wall outside, while I raced in with Lauren and found the bathroom. We were all starving too and I was delighted I'd remembered to bring a packed lunch. It was really intended to keep them sweet on the long journey, but because they slept, I hadn't required it. We devoured everything I'd packed, got changed and legged it down to the beach. We had the whole beach to ourselves on this fine, sunny afternoon in late October. We jumped over the waves and splashed each other, screaming and howling with glee the whole time. Henry must have heard us at the other end of the beach and I saw him sauntering towards us in the distance.

It was remarkable how helpful he was to me. The first thing he asked was whether we'd eaten. When I told him we ate every last morsel that I'd brought, he offered to go shopping for us. I wrote him a list and gave him some cash, while we all dried off at the cottage and had a proper look around. It was rustic and bare, but I didn't mind. It met our basic requirements of warmth, comfort and shelter. It was so remote too, I wasn't worried about Jeffrey finding us.

Henry arrived back a couple of hours later with our groceries. I cooked some nuggets, baked beans and frozen chips for dinner and everyone was happy. Henry also bought wine, which I hadn't ordered, and I declined. It wasn't going to be a night like that, I assured him. Not with the kids present. Anyway, this week was all about gaining clarity for me and I couldn't obtain that if I was drunk or hungover. He didn't push it and insisted it was his treat for some other time. I put it in the fridge, but seriously doubted I'd touch it this week.

I suggested he could take it and have it with Christine next time she came to visit, but he told me they'd broken up. She'd told him the caravan was a novelty place to stay for one weekend only, and not to call her until he'd built a house of his own, or bought one. I sympathised and told him she was a city girl and she'd probably prefer to date someone in a fixed abode rather than a mobile one.

'With all the money coming my way in these recent months, I'll have enough saved to build my own in a year. I have the site, near my parents' house, and there's plenty around here who owe me a favour or two. Mark my words, she'll be begging me to take her in this time next year.'

I was impressed with his confidence. We chatted a while longer and again, I made him promise not to tell Jeffrey where we were. The rest of the week was blissful, full of shell collecting, stone skimming and paddling in the roaring sea. The children were in their element.

Of course, I got dozens of phone calls from Jeffrey, worried sick and wondering what had gotten into me. He asked whether I'd lost my mind or was going through a midlife crisis. I only told him that we were all safe and well and I needed time away from him. He couldn't understand it and I had to hang up on him each time, because I didn't want to engage.

Henry took us out in the boat on one of the calmer, less windy afternoons. It was great fun initially, until Daniel started to feel sick. He passed his nausea on to the twins and all of a sudden it became apparent that we needed to disembark ASAP. As soon as we did, all three of them got sick and I knew they'd had enough adventure for one day. They were exhausted, so I put them to bed early. Henry offered to join me for a glass of wine once they were asleep, but I declined. He'd been so generous this week, I was actually worried what may happen if I let down my guard with him. He really was a kind soul, but I only liked him as a friend and reminded him of that every day. He was quite incorrigible, yet endearing at the same time.

'Ah, you don't mean that, Beatrice,' he'd say. 'I do, Henry, I really do,' I'd smile back, sympathetically. He took it well and we all had some fun times together in that special week. Until the last day, that is.

✧ ✧ ✧

WAS IT ME? Had I become a bit lax about the kids playing together on the beach? I'd been so careful for the first few days, watching their every movement and warning them of the rough sea, but then the weather became cooler and we stopped going into the sea. We stopped paddling too. We just collected a little water in our buckets, so we could make sandcastles. Then, we'd collect stones and shells to decorate them. It was the most mindful activity I'd ever done. We were just so focussed on creating the best castle ever.

I was helping Daniel, until he needed to go to the toilet. I brought him behind the rocks. There was no one around and it would have taken us a few minutes to get back to the cottage. I had wipes and tissues on me. We did that and when we got back, Lauren was trying to hide her sandcastle from us. We laughed and joined in and tried to hide ours from hers. We busied ourselves with the decoration for a few minutes, before I turned around again. My hunch was right. It was just Lauren.

'Where's Mia?' I shouted across the wind. No answer. I shouted louder. 'WHERE'S MIA?' Lauren looked up and pointed towards the ocean.

'I think she went to get water,' she said, absentmindedly. I looked to the sea. She wasn't there. I went down there to check, in case she'd fallen over or something. No sign of her. There was no sign of her. THERE WAS NO SIGN OF HER! I screamed her name. 'MIA! MIA!' But got no reply. I turned around towards Daniel and Lauren and ran to scoop them up in my arms. They both screamed and kicked. 'But what about my sandcastle?' they pleaded. I ran back to the cottage with them hanging out of my arms to get my phone and raise the alarm. I dialled emergency, 112, first and got through to the guards. I got the words out—'five-year-old missing on the beach. Went to fill her bucket with water and I took my eyes off her.' Something to that effect anyway.

Then, of course, I called Jeffrey. I had to.

Chapter Twenty One

'BEATRICE, BEATRICE, CALM down. You're not making sense. What do you mean, missing at sea?' he pleaded and begged me to tell him exactly what happened. It was only when he heard the sirens blaring in the background that he realised what sort of an emergency this was. I immediately told him where I was and to get directions from Henry once he arrived in Glan Mahogue. I relayed the events of the past fifteen minutes to the local guard, who was getting in touch with sea and air rescue. I wanted to go with them and search for her myself, but he insisted I stay with Daniel and Lauren. 'Let the emergency response team do their job. They're the professionals, not you. These two little ones need you right now. Is there anyone local you can call?' he asked.

'Henry,' I blurted out. 'Henry McCormack.'

'I'll get him for you,' said the guard. 'I'll get him right away. He's in *Get Fed*. I saw him there not twenty minutes ago.'

I got some hot milk and cookies for the kids

and tried to reassure them that the guards would find Mia. 'Everything will be okay,' I said, but each time I said it, I broke down crying. That set Daniel and Lauren off too, so that when Henry arrived, we were all huddled on the floor in bits.

He peeled the kids off me, sat them in front of the TV and turned on cartoons. He picked me up off the floor and as he did, I said, 'Jeffrey, Jeffrey. Did you speak to Jeffrey?'

'Of course I didn't,' he answered. 'Sure, you made it abundantly clear that I wasn't to tell him anything.'

His stupidity did nothing but compound my torture. 'You're making this worse, Henry! You're making it worse!' I screamed at him.

We rang Jeffrey immediately and told him exactly where to go. One of his new celebrity friends had offered him a private jet, so he said he'd be in Glan Mahogue within the hour. I sent Henry out to join the search party. He made me a cup of tea first and sat me on the couch with the kids, still sipping their hot milk, totally engrossed in *Nelly and Nora*. It was one of my favourites too, so we sat together and watched one after the other. It seemed to be a *Nelly and Nora* marathon.

I looked out the window, when the cartoons eventually ended. There was no sign of relief or no one shouting that they'd found her. I dropped to my knees in disbelief that this could be happening.

Lauren came to my rescue. 'C'mon Mammy, over here on the couch. Look, *Bing* is starting.' I let her lead me to the couch. Daniel looked as though he was nodding off, so I sat him on my lap and wrapped my arms around both of them. We just waited. We sat there and waited.

I found *Bing* to be just as comforting as *Nelly and Nora*. Why didn't I sit down more and cuddle my kids on the couch while watching their favourite cartoons? Why didn't I ever think of doing this? I was a bad, selfish mother, always thinking of myself and furthering my career. I didn't focus enough on these…these little angels. I wiped more tears from my face, just with my sleeve. I didn't want to get up for a tissue and upset our cosy entanglement on the couch. Daniel fell asleep on my lap and Lauren handed me a tissue. I forgot that Jeffrey always made sure their pockets were full of tissues. He taught them how to wipe their noses and blow them properly too. In fact, most of what they know was taught to them by him. What did I do for them? What did I contribute to this family?

No wonder Jeffrey had his sights set on someone else. Someone more capable and accomplished than me and no doubt Linda was. She was a doctor, so therefore highly intelligent. She probably loved kids too and…I couldn't. I couldn't go on with this line of thinking. It was breaking me. It was just me creating distractions in my mind to escape from what was actually happening. My little girl could have drowned in the wild Atlantic ocean. She could be floating away to America by now.

Or maybe she found a rock. A big, hard, consolidated mound of bedrock that burst through the ocean floor in the shape of a little armchair for her to curl up in and wait for the rescue team.

Who was I kidding? The ocean was vicious and wild. It would be a miracle if they found her alive. But why did none of us hear her screams? We weren't that far away. Surely, she would have yelled in fright if the waves swept her in? I turned to Lauren.

'Honey, was she definitely going to get water for the sandcastle? Did you see her?'

'I saw her walking down with the yellow bucket, but I didn't see her come back. You see, I was putting the little stones around the edges and making shapes and...'

'Okay, okay, darling. It's okay. They'll find her. They know what they're doing.' My phone rang and Daniel stirred. I reached over him and picked it up from the coffee table.

'Jeffrey, where are you?'

'Is that Daddy? Is that Daddy?' Lauren got excited.

'I'm walking up the beach now. I've just been

talking to a member of the Air and Sea Rescue team. They're sending divers in now.'

'Now? Only now? She's been missing for nearly an hour and they're only searching the sea now?' I started to panic. I thought they'd be in there already, pulling her out.

'They sent in surface swimmers, but they didn't find her.' He paused and choked on those words. 'Oh God, Beatrice, where is she?'

'Hang on, Jeffrey.'

I lifted sleepy Daniel onto the couch and Lauren came with me. We opened the door and saw Jeffrey approaching with Mia's little yellow bucket.

'That's it! That's it!' Lauren squealed. 'That's the one she was trying to fill!'

I put my hand over my mouth and felt as though I'd been struck by lightning. The shock of seeing the bucket, the last thing she'd clung to. It was too much for me. I collapsed on the spot and Jeffrey ran to pick me up.

'Mammy! Mammy!' Lauren yelled, waking Daniel in the process. Jeffrey brought me inside, sat me down and then gathered the two children in his arms on the floor and kissed them wildly, telling them how much he loved them and missed them. I looked at the three of them and realised that everything that had just happened was all my fault. I was intrinsically flawed as a human being and should never have been allowed to give birth. One should have to pass a test to be granted the privilege of motherhood. I would have failed it miserably. Look what I'd done. I took my eyes off her on one of the most dangerous, stoniest, rockiest beaches in the world. And on a wild, windy day too. How could I? What was wrong with me?

Jeffrey got up and made some toast. He buttered it and sliced it into little triangles, just the way the kids liked it and handed it to them.

'Here, there's some for you too.' He left a plate on the table. 'I'm going out to look for her. You stay here and mind these two, okay?'

I stared at him blankly.

'Beatrice! Eat this! You need some energy! You have to mind the children!' I'd never heard him sound so cross.

'Yes, yes, okay, I will.' Once he got a response from me, he shot out the door. Lauren and Daniel ran to the window to look at him.

'Is Daddy going to find Mia?' Daniel asked.

'Of course he is, you silly sausage!' Lauren replied and tickled him in the tummy. He dropped his toast laughing at her. I stayed at the window and was overwhelmed with what I saw. The whole population of Glan Mahogue were out scouring the beach. I recognised the postman, the local grocer, the barman from *The Shed*, the teacher who'd helped us fill in a questionnaire for the project and an elderly couple, who reminded me of Henry, so I assumed they were probably his parents. Jeffrey was down there frantically talking to the guard. He was pointing every which way and eventually set off in one direction.

There was a chance, I thought. Maybe a chance that she didn't actually get swept away by the ocean. Even despite finding the yellow bucket floating in there didn't put me off the thought. The fact that we didn't hear her holler was confusing me. I thought of the photo shoot and how the models yelled every time the water splashed them. Mia would have screamed too if a wave hit her. She would have screeched very loudly with the sheer coldness of it. And she was loud. She had the loudest, strongest wail of the three of them. But we heard no sound. Nothing. It didn't make sense. I felt I needed to tell someone. I rang Jeffrey. I told him to tell the rescue team that we heard nothing, when we should have heard screams. It was obvious he thought I was clutching at straws, but said he would tell them nonetheless. Just as I hung up on him, my phone rang.

'Henry! Not now!' I snapped. I wanted my phone to be free for the emergency team, when they rang to tell me they'd found her. I didn't want Henry bugging me.

It beeped again and I realised the damn thing

was out of batteries. How could I let that happen? I cursed myself. I scrambled around looking for the charger, while Lauren and Daniel were still rolling around tickling each other and laughing.

I suddenly got a pang and wondered would Daniel even remember her? He was only three years old. Would he remember his sister Mia if the worst happened. And Lauren. What would it be like for her to lose a twin? They did everything together. They were in the same class in school. They shared the same friends. They liked the same food. They often got confused and used each other's toothbrushes, because they insisted on the same ones. They were like an extension of each other and for Lauren, I could only imagine it would be like losing her right arm. And her best friend. Her sister. Her twin.

Shit! Where was my charger? I looked out the window, but nothing had changed. No one was calling me or looking for my attention. They knew where I was.

I found it. It was in the drawer in my bedroom. I brought it out to the kitchen and plugged it in. I switched on my phone and noticed my hand shaking as I punched in the code. It vibrated immediately, alerting me to messages. I raced to the front door, but no one was looking my way. I went back to the phone and discovered the missed calls were from Henry. He rang back. Why would he do that? He knew what was going on.

Then it struck me that he must know something. He'd only ring more than twice if it was super important. My phone sounded again, just as I held it in my hand. I saw it was Henry. I answered, but said nothing. I just held the phone to my ear, so he could speak.

Chapter Twenty Two

'I FOUND HER,' he said.

'You what?'

'I said I found her.'

Silence. I wasn't sure what to...

'Beatrice, can you hear me? I found her and she's okay.'

'She's okay? Are you sure?'

'I found her in my caravan. You know how I always leave it unlocked? She must have wandered away on the beach. Here, here, she wants to talk to you.'

'Mammy? Mammy? Is that you?'

'Mia! Mia! You're okay?'

'Yes, and I found Henry's caravan all by myself!' She sounded delighted with herself. Then, I heard voices in the background. I think I recognised Jeffrey's. The next voice who spoke was his. He took the phone off Mia.

'She's here. She's safe. I have her in my arms.'

Then, there were more background voices. It was Henry shouting. 'Call it off! Call it off! We found her!'

I dropped the phone, totally by accident. When I picked it up, it was cut off. 'Shit!' I shouted and attempted to ring back. Straight to voicemail.

'Did Mammy say shit?' I overheard Lauren asking Daniel.

'Quick, guys! Get your coats on! We're going to see Mia! Now!'

'Mia? Where is she? Where are we going?' Lauren was ecstatic.

I smiled at both of them. 'Henry's caravan!'

'Yay!' They clapped and cheered. It dawned on me that they'd heard all about Henry's caravan when they interrogated him on the first day about where he lived. He'd made promises to show it to them, but we never made it down that far on the beach. I was also worried Jeffrey might have someone in Glan Mahogue looking out for us and Henry's caravan would be the first place they'd look. I suppose I'd kind of been avoiding going anywhere for fear of being caught. Henry did our shopping for us, so we didn't venture far from the cottage all week.

The guard I'd spoken with was still on the beach and he gave me a huge smile and a thumbs up as we ran past him as fast as our legs would carry us.

'Ar nós na gaoithe!' Lauren called out as we raced by him. She had just learned that in school in her Irish lesson. 'Like the wind', it meant, and it was apt at this moment, because we all ran like the wind. We were being carried by the wind, in fact. Maybe the wind had guided Mia on her ramble up the beach earlier. Carried her to safety though, rather than to death like we'd all feared.

It was a good wind.

✧ ✧ ✧

SUDDENLY, I STOPPED in my tracks. Lauren and Daniel ran on, waving and screaming. 'It's Mia! Look, there she is!' I'd never seen Daniel run so hard and fast before. The sea air on the west coast must have built up his leg muscles and maybe seeing his beloved sister in the distance had strengthened his resolve.

I let them go. I had to stop. I couldn't breathe. The sight of Jeffrey on one side, holding hands with Mia, and Henry on the other side waving frantically at us—it was too much. It took my breath away and I couldn't catch it. I had to stop. I bent over, thinking a rush of blood to my head might help. I peeled myself up slowly, like I used to in yoga class. It worked. I took a breath. It enabled me to carry on. I walked this time. I couldn't seem to run anymore. I made a mental note to resume yoga. All that breathing and tuning into your body might just help me now. At least, it wouldn't do any harm. It was abundantly clear I'd need some life hacks to survive from here on, but right now all I wanted was cuddles from Mia.

And that's what I got.

✧ ✧ ✧

HENRY MENTIONED THAT he had 7 Up in the fridge, so we all piled into his little caravan and he produced some plastic cups that he kept on reserve for unexpected guests. I'd heard stories about crowds gathering in Henry's caravan or around it, weather permitting, either before or after booze ups in *The Shed*. It seemed to be a community meeting point of sorts.

It was a tight squeeze for four people around the dining table. I perched on a low folding stool, Jeffrey sat Daniel on his lap and Henry hovered, at hand for refills. He had some jellies that he'd been planning to give the kids for their journey home tomorrow. The three of them were high as kites on a sugar buzz and when Henry refilled Lauren's 7 Up, she exclaimed, 'THIS IS THE BEST DAY EVER!' Everyone's first reaction was to laugh, but this was followed by gulps and teary eyes from me and Jeffrey. It was hard to swallow and we choked up. I wanted to reach for him, but Daniel and Lauren were like a barrier between us. I wondered if Jeffrey wanted it that way.

Then, Mia decided to explain how she ended up in Henry's caravan. We were all ears.

'I tried to fill the yellow bucket, but I lost it and saw it drifting off. I thought Lauren would be mad at me, 'cause it's her bucket, so I went up the hill to get some of the little stones for her. She likes the little pebbles.'

'Yeah, I love them.' Lauren nodded and wholeheartedly corroborated her sister's story. Mia continued.

'I was really good at climbing and when I got to the top of the hill...'

'The cliff edge,' Henry innocently corrected her and I saw Jeffrey's eyes widen. He was going to kill me later for this. I could tell.

'Yeah, the cliff, I saw your caravan!' She beamed. 'So, then I ran and ran and ran, 'cause I wanted to be the first to get to your caravan! And I made it!'

We all gave her a clap, even though it felt so wrong. Soooo wrong.

'And the door was open and I needed to go to the toilet. Then, I decided to play house.' She got up to demonstrate, pointing to various objects to embellish her story. 'So, this was my kitchen and this was my bedroom and this was my living room and this was my play area.' She just sat on a little mat in the middle of the floor.

'Mia,' I asked. 'Didn't you hear the sirens outside on the beach?'

'Yeah, I did,' she said. 'They were very noisy and I didn't like them, so I closed the door. It was kind of distracting me from my game.' Then, Lauren got up. 'Can I play?' she asked. And of course, Daniel hopped out of Jeffrey's lap. 'Me too! Can I play? I'll be the daddy. You be the mammy and Lauren can be the baby.'

Jeffrey got up. 'Beatrice, outside for a minute.' We let them play together on the floor, as Henry opened another bag of jellies. 'For the game,' he chuckled.

Myself and Jeffrey walked down to the beach. We saw the last of the emergency rescue team leaving. Mortification rose in me as I considered all the drama I'd caused. I had a little cry into my hands. Jeffrey just stood there and waited for me to finish. He handed me a tissue. Always had a tissue on him.

'Thanks,' I said.

'Beatrice, I don't even know where to begin.' He shook his head. Then, his phone rang. It was the pilot, telling him he'd be taking off shortly and heading back to Dublin. Jeffrey thanked him, saying he was planning to drive back.

'Beatrice, how could you let this happen? Look at the sea! Look at those waves! I've never seen anything like it. So thunderous and wild and you let our five-year-old down there on her own? Even the stones and shells could have cut her feet. What were you thinking?' I'd never seen him so mad.

'She had...she had her runners on.' He just looked at me, wide eyed and speechless. He waited for me to explain myself.

'All week', I started, 'I didn't take my eyes off them all week, I promise. We were so careful. They weren't allowed to go near the water unless either myself or Henry was with them.'

'Henry? Did you put him in charge of our kids?' He was getting angrier. I could see the tension in his eyes and for the first time ever, I noticed lines on his forehead. He wouldn't like that. He was not a fan of ageing, especially visible ageing.

'No, just when we went out on his boat, just that time.'

'You let him take the kids out on his rotting, decrepit, obviously not seaworthy boat? Am I hearing you correctly?'

'Is it rotting? Not seaworthy? I didn't know! I trusted him. He goes out fishing in it every day.'

He took a deep breath. 'Tell me now, why was she filling up her bucket of water on her own? Where were you?'

'I...I...we were having a sandcastle competition. It was me and Daniel against the girls. Then, Daniel needed to go to the toilet, so I brought him around behind the rocks and when we got back, we didn't notice straight away that Mia wasn't there. I guess Lauren was intent on decorating her castle and it was probably a few minutes before I clocked that Mia wasn't with her.' I paused to take a breath. It was still raw. It felt too soon to be reliving it. I continued when I was ready.

'Then, when I asked Lauren where Mia was, she said refilling the bucket. That's when I panicked and rang the emergency services. Oh no, actually, I didn't have my phone on me, so we had to run back to the cottage to get it, so it was a few minutes later that I actually rang.' I looked down, disgusted with myself. He seemed to be trying to get his head around how I could have let this happen. The children never even grazed their knees under his watch. He was always so attentive towards them. His parental supremacy only served to highlight my shortcomings and make me feel worse.

Relief swept through me when we were interrupted by Henry.

'Beatrice!' he roared. 'Mia says she's starving.'

I looked at Jeffrey. We'd have to continue this later. I ran back to collect the three children, while Jeffrey sat on a rock and shivered. I hugged Henry. I actually didn't know if or when I'd ever see him again. He knew it too and hugged me back with vigour.

'Goodbye, Beatrice,' he whispered in my ear. I

tried to thank him and say goodbye, but words wouldn't come out and I just attempted to wipe away the tears streaming down my face. I was filled with conflicting emotions. I didn't know how I felt about Glan Mahogue, about this caravan before me, about the wild, roaring Atlantic Ocean or about Henry. I just wanted to focus on Mia and look after her and the other two. Beyond that, I didn't know.

I just didn't know.

Chapter Twenty Three

When everyone was fed and our belongings packed up, we got into the car for the long drive home. Jeffrey drove. He was silently going through the motions, except to instruct the children. He barely looked at me. After about an hour of constant motion, the children fell asleep, one by one. I saw them as I checked my mirror and discreetly looked back, not wanting to disturb them. Each one's head fell very slowly to one side, mouth open and eyes closed with purpose. I was sure they must've been exhausted and felt confident they'd sleep until we got home.

'She's just gone,' I whispered to Jeffrey, when Lauren was the last to drop off. He didn't answer. 'Jeffrey, we can talk now. They're all asleep.'

'Well then, go ahead. Talk! Tell me why you vanished with the kids without warning and left me on my own. Tell me, Beatrice, because I have no idea.'

'Really? I don't believe you. You must know why, Jeffrey. You must!'

'How would I know? My life, our lives have been crazy these past few months. I feel like I'm on a treadmill trying to keep everything running smoothly. And I thought I was managing, but obviously not.' He kept his eye on the road the whole time and didn't look my way at all.

'Jeffrey, I can't believe I even have to explain. I wish you'd just own up and be done with this.'

'What are you talking about, Bea? Tell me what you know or what you think you know.'

'I know you're seeing Linda again.'

That's all I said. He remained silent. I turned to look at him. He loosened his grip on the wheel before tightening it again. He did this a few times to flex his hands. He was seriously stressed. I'd ruffled him. I could tell. Neither of us spoke again and then, out of the blue, he pulled off the road into an exit.

'Oh, do we need petrol?' I asked.

'I don't know,' he answered. He parked in a spot, took off his seatbelt and turned towards me.

'So, you mean all of this, the whole week of torture you've just put me through was because you thought I was back with Linda?'

I'd never heard him so heated. I thought earlier today was the angriest I'd ever seen him, but I was wrong. He was scaring me.

'Jeffrey, stop! You'll wake the kids.' I turned around to check on them, but they hadn't stirred.

'Answer me, Beatrice! Did you really think that?'

'Not think—I KNOW you've been seeing her. I know, Jeffrey!'

'What are you talking about?'

'I saw a message on your screen in your office from her. I saw her name and recognised her profile picture attached. So, you see, I know. I have the proof, so there's no use in denying it!'

He turned away from me and put his head in his hands. He seemed to need a minute before continuing.

'You didn't open the message, did you?' he said, half under his breath.

'No, of course not. I would never invade your privacy like that. The only reason I saw the message at all was because the notification beeped while I was in there looking for dirty laundry in your gym basket. I wasn't prying or spying. It just caught my attention when it beeped.'

'I wish you did,' he whispered.

'What? What did you just say, Jeffrey?'

'I wish you'd opened it. Or better still, asked me about it.'

'Why? So you could concoct more lies like last time?' I said, accusingly.

'I never lied to you the last time. I confessed everything when the time was right. I was as honest as possible with you.'

'When the time was right! WHEN THE TIME WAS RIGHT!' Now it was me shouting. I saw him look back at the kids. 'You confessed everything when SHE dumped you! How's that for timing? What if she hadn't dumped you? You'd still be with her!'

'No, no that's not true. It was a relief when she ended it. I said this at therapy. Don't you remember? I couldn't live with the deceit any longer.'

'Looks like it didn't stop you this time round,' I snapped back.

He sat back and sighed deeply. 'I can't do this now,' he said. 'I'd better get us all home in one piece.' He turned to look at the sleeping trio. 'Get these kids tucked up in bed.' Then, he looked at me. 'We'll talk later. I mean, really talk. Get it all out in the open.'

He moved the car over to a tank, filled up with petrol and stuck in his Lady Gaga CD. It was abundantly clear he was done talking to me. Come to think of it, maybe he was just done with me, full stop.

✧ ✧ ✧

THEY DIDN'T WAKE when we carried them in from the car. Mia stirred a little when I pulled up the covers on her bed, so I just knelt by her side and rubbed her forehead until she settled. In the meantime, Jeffrey unpacked the car. I wanted to help him, but found I couldn't. I couldn't tear myself away from Mia's bedside. Tears rolled down my cheeks as I looked at the rise and fall of her innocent breath. Silent tears. I barely even registered that I was crying, only I scratched my nose and discovered my face was wet.

Jeffrey found me. I don't know how long I'd been kneeling there looking at her. He whispered, 'Beatrice, she's asleep. You can leave her be.' He offered his hand to help me up and I took it. He led me out to the landing. 'Look at you, you're exhausted. You need to rest.'

'But, Jeffrey, we need to talk, don't we? We need to...'

'Shush. Yes, we definitely do, but you're pale and ghostly. You really need to go to bed.' I didn't argue with him. I'd been to hell and back today and I was truly wiped. I rubbed away some more tears and he called me. 'Here', he said and handed me a sachet of Beauty Lane's signature cleanser. 'Use this to cleanse and then get some sleep, okay?'

✧ ✧ ✧

THE NEXT DAY Jeffrey got up early with the children. I slept in until 10 am, which was super late for me. I went downstairs in my dressing gown to get morning cuddles. I craved affection from the kids since yesterday's catastrophe and kept thinking what might have been and how lucky we were. Jeffrey was cooking pancakes for breakfast, so everyone was in a great mood.

'Mammy, when can we go back to that beach and Henry's caravan?' Mia asked. She really wanted to continue her game of 'house'.

'Not for a while, I'm afraid. It's a very long journey and school's back tomorrow!'

In the end, Jeffrey promised to buy a playhouse for them out the back garden so they could continue to play 'house'. When they saw the pictures of the potential playhouses online, they stopped asking about Henry's caravan and insisted he make the purchase straight away. He laughed and said we might all go shopping later on. I caught his eye and he nodded. He set them up with colouring books and crayons at the kitchen table after breakfast and gestured to me that we should go into his office. We left the door open, so we'd hear the kids if they needed us.

I sat on the high makeup stool and he turned on his computer. 'What are you doing? I thought we were going to talk.' He was confusing me now. I actually wondered if he had divorce documents ready to show me or something. Why was he switching on his computer? He turned his back and ignored me while he typed and eventually opened a document for me to see. It was an advertisement for 'Dr Linda Craven and Associates'. When I saw her image on the screen, I said, 'That's her, isn't it? I was right!'

Then he typed some more and opened a thread of messages. He helped me off the stool and asked me to read them. I looked at the screen and said, 'But Jeffrey, these are your private messages. I can't.' I saw the subject heading and it read 'Private and Confidential'.

'Just do it, really. You have my full consent.' I looked at the screen and scrolled down as I read through.

Dear Jeffrey,

I am forwarding you this message I received from Dr Jean Lafferty. I understand you contacted her regarding anxiety and profuse perspiration since beginning a new career. She has referred you to see me, as I am the leading anxiety coach here in my practice.

However, given our past (and I'm trying to keep this as professional as possible), I think it would be better if I made a further referral for you to meet with one of my esteemed colleagues instead.

I trust you will understand and if you have any further queries, please don't hesitate to contact the clinic.

I wish you well, Jeffrey.

Regards,
Dr Linda Craven.

He scrolled down to show me his reply. I just

stood there, stunned and speechless. I read on.

Dear Linda,

I didn't realise my request would reach you, although I was aware this is your area of expertise. I think you're doing the right thing in referring me to one of your colleagues, but I also know you're the best in the business when it comes to treating people battling stress and anxiety.

Just to further inform you and your colleague, I wanted to elaborate on the specific, work-related obstacles I'm facing.

As you may or may not know, I have recently changed my career direction and winning a nationwide competition has catapulted me into the public eye. There are new demands on me such as interviews, TV appearances and photo shoots. Normally, I'm a very confident person, as you may remember, but it has unnerved me of late how anxious I've been getting pre appearances and interviews. I've been sweating excessively and have to change my shirt at least three times a day. I've noticed a shake in my hand, which I never had before and my throat goes so dry, it inhibits my speech, which can be highly embarrassing if I'm mid interview.

However, the worst element of my

symptoms is my racing heart. I've always prided myself in staying calm amid stressful situations, but there's something about a camera pointing towards me that sets me off. My heart rate goes into overdrive and I've often thought I might be having a heart attack. It's definitely related to when I see the 'Live' green light on the camera and I know I have to speak, or perform even.

I'm hopeful you and your associates can help me in a professional capacity. Obviously, it wouldn't be appropriate for you to work alongside me, given our history, but I wanted you to have the full picture so you can select the right person to help me. I know I can trust your organisation and I'll get the best treatment under your care.

I hope it's okay to personally reply to you like this. I just want to ensure you match me up with the correct doctor and/or therapist. I'm suffering with shame and embarrassment. I'm desperate to get on top of this and I know you can help.

Yours sincerely,
Jeffrey Walsh.

I scrolled down this time to see her reply. I noted the time and date. I guess this was the one that popped up on screen when I was looking for the dirty clothes.

Dear Jeffrey,

I admire you for diagnosing your symptoms so early on. You know, some people live with these crippling symptoms for years before they seek help. I commend you for acting so soon.

I can definitely recommend a therapist to work with you. I will book you in for an initial consultation at your convenience.

Congratulations on your newfound fame! I've seen your image in magazines and newspapers. Exciting times and I wish you well! I'm also glad you patched things up with your wife. I saw you were photographed together recently. It was obviously meant to be. I have moved on also—I just thought you might like to know.

I will now send an email from the company address and attach an application form for you and a booking request. I will pass this on to a suitable therapist, one who is highly qualified to help you with your issues and we will end our contact with each other.

I wish you well, Jeffrey, and thank you for choosing Linda Craven and Associates.

Kind regards,
Linda.

Chapter Twenty Four

HE REALISED I'D finished reading and then opened the application and booking form he'd filled out. I put my hand over my mouth. I was in shock. I rubbed my face and scratched my messy head.

'So you…you're not back together with her? I thought…oh.' I dropped my head. My mind was racing. So, they're not back together. I've misread the whole thing. This past…this past week was…all for nothing. *I don't…I just don't believe it.* I continued scratching my head in confusion.

'No, Beatrice. You've just read every bit of contact I've had with Linda. It's all above board, I can assure you. I just used her as a go-between to get the help I needed. There was no way I was trying to rekindle anything.'

I looked at him. Deep into his eyes. And, shit, I believed him. We remained in silence for a few minutes while I came to terms with my mistake. But hang on…he knowingly corresponded with his ex. He reached out to her with full disclosure of his personal ailments. He looked for attention from HER. I couldn't condone this, despite feeling like a fool for jumping to conclusions.

It was like he was waiting for me to say something, but he got in before me.

'You don't trust me, do you?' he offered. It sounded like an accusation. It was. That's exactly what it was and I was stumped. I didn't know what to say and I didn't want to say the wrong thing.

'Well? It's true, isn't it? You don't trust me,' he carried on.

I put my head down and whimpered, 'Em, no, I don't think I do.'

'Well, that's it, then. I mean, we can't go on from here, can we?'

That's it? THAT'S IT?! He was leaving me? It's not like I thought. This was not at all the way I thought it would be. He wasn't leaving me to shack up with Linda or a young model. He was leaving me because he thought I was the one in the wrong. I'm the one with trust issues. Granted I acted in an irrational manner. I should have just confronted him straight away when I found the message from Linda. Damn it! If I'd done that, Mia wouldn't have had her near accident at sea and the emergency services wouldn't have had to waste unnecessary time searching for her. I accepted I was hasty and got carried away with jealousy. I accepted that and thought I could find it within to forgive myself for it.

But in a way he has betrayed me once again. In contacting his former lover, it showed a lack of regard for me, his wife. I couldn't ignore this. Even after all the drama this past week, I couldn't overlook the fact that Jeffrey interacted with his ex behind my back.

I pulled my gaze upwards to look him in the eye.

'Are you saying you're going to leave me, Jeffrey? Is that what you're implying?' This time I sounded like the accusatory one. There was even a mild sense of threat in my tone and he clocked it.

He stepped back. 'Wait, what? Now I'm the one in trouble? After everything you put this family through this week? You're getting antsy with me?' He was sweating now, with anger in his eyes. I paused before responding. *God bless my newly learned communicative tools.*

'Yes, you're right. I am getting antsy. I know I've done wrong by dashing off with the kids. I should have stayed and told you I'd seen that message on your computer. I see that now. Believe me, I do. I'm annoyed with myself, but I'm also annoyed with you. I tried to reach out to you for weeks on end about your standoffish behaviour and moodiness, but you fobbed me off.'

'No, that's not true, I...'

'Yes, Jeffrey. It IS true. I remember. I was even considering returning to couple's counselling to get you to open up to me. I knew something was wrong. And, now I find out you'd rather share your troubles with your ex lover than discuss them with me, your wife. How do you think that makes me feel?'

He took a step back, perplexed. He clearly wasn't expecting me to hold him accountable like this, but I stood my ground. I stood up for myself in a way that I hadn't done previously. Truth and fairness were fundamental to me and I was reminded of our simulated debate night in the communications class. Back then, I was defending country living as opposed to city life—a topic thrown out to us from our course facilitator. But now, I was defending honesty, openness and marital trust—everything that was important to me.

We stood in silence for a while before looking up and locking eyes. Eventually, he spoke.

'When I said "we can't go on like this", I meant we can't continue this cycle of mistrust between us. I didn't mean it to sound like I was going to leave you.'

'Oh,' I said. Phew, I thought. He continued.

'I thought the counselling was enough last year, but obviously it wasn't enough for you.' He scrunched his eyes like he was agonised by his current train of thought. 'How pompous of me to think I could win your trust back with a few sessions of counselling? You needed more. Of course you did. I see that now.'

Yes. Yessss, this was exactly what I needed to hear right now.

'I was the one who broke our marriage vows and I don't deserve your trust anymore. Everything that happened this week, it's on me just as much as you.' He stopped to move closer to me. Our eyes were still locked with intensity. He brushed his hand down my cheek. Was this really happening? I wondered. Was he really saying all these things? This felt like communication on another level. As a couple, we weren't used to this, but I think I'd LIKE to get used to it. A tiny smile escaped through my lips. It was one of relief that there was hope for us. Real, tangible progress was being made as we edged closer in mutual relief.

He spoke so quietly it was almost a whisper. 'Look, it's clear you should have asked me about the message you saw from Linda, but at the same time, I SHOULD have thought to tell you that I was in contact with her. I see that now and I have to take my share of the blame.'

He stared into my eyes. He was so close to me, I could smell him—that Jeffrey smell. Like lavender it was. It must be in the scented moisturiser he was using. I inhaled it. Lavender made me relax.

'Jeffrey, this all comes back to our communication. We both need to up our game and open up more. Were you too embarrassed to tell me about your perspiration problems? And, the palpitations. They must have been scaring you senseless.' I reached up and stroked his cheek. It felt warm. He'd been sweating.

He stepped back to look at me before replying. 'That's why I went to a professional. I thought I could work through it on my own without letting anyone know, but I suppose I should have taken the time to discuss it with you. I don't know. I didn't want to appear weak or something. I wanted you to think I had everything under control.'

'Because you usually do?'

'Yeah, I guess. I was trying to protect my new career too. I thought if you knew I was struggling, you might want me to step back or pack it in altogether and I wasn't ready to give up just yet. You know I've felt like you weren't 100% behind me with this new direction. Are you...are you embarrassed of me or something? Or worried I won't be able to provide for the family? My job in IT was definitely a more stable career choice.'

'No, no, Jeffrey. None of those things. I'm proud of you for making these huge changes and throwing yourself fully into the fashion world. I could see you were out of your comfort zone on occasion and sensed your unease, but I didn't want to draw attention to it, in case it stressed you further. You know, if you thought you looked stressed, you might feel it more. Does that make sense?'

He chuckled. 'Yeah, I think I know what you mean.'

'So, what did you mean earlier when you said we can't go on like this? How do you propose we 'go on'?'

'We need help. We need therapy and not the same one as last time. She let us go before you were ready to trust me again. We need a better therapist, a more informed one. And I'm going to find us one.'

I looked at him and smiled. 'I trust you to do that!'

It was abundantly clear we had a long road ahead. We would both need to find a way to forgive me for taking my eyes off Mia on such a dangerous beach. I would have to learn to trust Jeffrey wholly and completely, because he was right. Our marriage wouldn't endure a lack of belief on my part. It just wouldn't survive unless I learned to trust him again. But it was a two-way street. He would have to believe that he could confide in me. First and foremost, I was his number one confidante and I wanted him to be abundantly clear of that...and place his trust in me.

✧ ✧ ✧

IF I'D LEARNED anything in recent months, it was that methodical communication strategies were the way forward for me. I endeavoured to implement them in every aspect of my life, both private and personal.

At uni I was experiencing breakthrough after breakthrough with successfully reaching my students. We were communicating, both in lectures and after hours. They would knock on my office door or catch me in the library if they had questions. I listened attentively and interacted with them like I had never done before. I used to just walk away, thinking no one was interested. But I was wrong—at least 50% of my students seemed to possess a love of geography equal to my own and it made my job more fulfilling and meaningful. That said, the time it took to reach this smooth transfer with the students was eating into my family life, so I began plotting how to create a more efficient work-life balance.

Now that Jeffrey's hours were somewhat erratic, I was required for the day-to-day running of the household. The grandparents were lending a hand with picking up the kids, but we didn't want to ask too much of them. They had their own hectic social lives in the active retirement community and we didn't want to take advantage. Jeffrey hung on to the things he loved best, like cooking family dinners and dropping the kids to school in the morning. But I was still trying desperately to strike some sort of balance. The possibility of job-sharing as a lecturer and only working part-time hours was becoming increasingly appealing to me.

For there was a new ambition quietly festering within since I got the results of my communications course and the facilitator's feedback. She was very encouraging and some of her suggestions gave me food for thought. I'd need to discuss it first with Jeffrey of course. I wasn't going to embark on anything without his full blessing.

That was another positive outcome of my communications course. Not only did it make me a more effective lecturer, but it also gave me the tools to become an immersive communicator with Jeffrey. It made me a better wife! I didn't reply to his texts haphazardly anymore, which used to frustrate him to no end. I made my point and stated it clearly and concisely to avoid confusion. I even read it first to myself to make sure it made sense before I sent it. I was no longer a passive listener in our late evening chats when the kids were sleeping. I was actively engaged, which wasn't difficult, because his news was always thrilling from the fashion world, not to mention the gossip from behind closed doors at the TV station. It was exciting to hear what the celebs were REALLY like, but I had to swear not to breathe a word of this classified information to anyone.

Jeffrey also decided to turn down work if it

involved extensive travel or very late nights. He was still in demand, so he had flexibility to pick and choose. We both made sure to keep every Wednesday night free for our combined therapy session. It wasn't always focussed upon our relationship and mending our trust issues. Sometimes it was related to Jeffrey's anxiety about going on camera or my post-traumatic feelings after almost losing Mia at sea. I still had nightmares.

THERE WERE ALSO a few loose ends to tie up with the rock study. It got neglected with the busyness of a new term beginning, as these projects often do. Many get left by the wayside, but I pushed for this one, not wanting my hard work to go unnoticed. I didn't want to return to Glan Mahogue, though. I couldn't face the scene where my Mia went missing. It was too soon for me to revisit the beach. I encouraged Mr. Keel to take a trip with his wife. He contacted Henry while he was there. I had lost touch with him. I suppose he was another reminder of Mia's near fatal accident.

When Mr. Keel returned, he called me into his office.

Chapter Twenty Five

'BEATRICE! YOU NEVER told me our rock study contact was such a mad man!'

'Oh no, I should have warned you. What did he do?' I asked, with bated breath.

'Well, I met him in *The Shed* and we had a drink. Then, he invited myself and my wife back to his place for dinner. They don't serve food in *The Shed*. Liquid lunches only.'

'Yes, I know. But isn't there a restaurant next door? *Get Fed* or something?'

'It's closed for refurbishment. They're adding a new bakery, called *Eat Bread*. It's behind *Get Fed*, beside *The Bed*, which is joined onto *The Shed*. Then a little book shop for tourists has opened on the other side.'

'Oh? I hadn't heard,' I replied.

'Yes, it's called *Well Read* and it has information leaflets on the local beaches, flora and fauna, fishing spots and a detailed map of the locality. Tourists are flocking there apparently, so it's much needed.'

'Oh, how wonderful, I suppose. Although, I hope it doesn't get too built up. It's such a quaint little spot, isn't it?'

'Yes, very remote. I hope its popularity doesn't bring too much development to the town, although it's so remote, I can't imagine they'd build many houses there. But back to my story. My wife got dressed up for evening dinner at Henry's place and he picked us up from our hotel so we could have a glass of wine with dinner.'

'Okay...and?' It didn't sound too bad so far.

'Well, he brought us to a shack on the cliffedge and served fried fish on paper plates paired with the most disgusting, cheap bottle of wine that tasted like toilet water!'

'Let me guess, was it sauvignon blanc by any chance?' I actually didn't think it was that bad, but I guess I'd been drinking it more out of necessity than pleasure. And more from the perspective of a midlife crisis victim than a wine connoisseur.

'Yes, bought from *The Shed,* he informed us. My wife spat it out, it was so rank. Then, Henry asked me to send another rep from the geography department to extend and diversify the project. He very indelicately requested an unmarried, young female. Beatrice, do you know what this is about?'

'Oh, I think he's looking for a girlfriend and he tends to be a bit of a flirt.'

'And did he act in an untoward manner with

you?'

Gulp. Oh Jesus. I don't think I was the picture of respectability while I was there. I drank two bottles of wine, ran around the beach like a lunatic, ate my dinner and his, and had indecent relations with him in his love shack! No, I couldn't tell Mr. Keel any of this. I had to remind myself that I'm a professional and the truth would not be acceptable to Mr. Keel at this precise moment in time. So, I channelled my all-encompassing, actively engaged expressions that I'd learned in my communications course and replied to my esteemed boss and mentor.

'No. I can assure you, sir, he was a perfect gentleman.'

It seemed my response was more than adequate for Mr. Keel and he said he wouldn't strike Henry off our list of contacts just yet.

'Besides,' he added, 'my wife found him very charming and he invited her down next month for a local festival, where they're honouring him as Mayor of Glan Mahogue.'

'Really? Mayor? And is she going?'

'Yes, but unfortunately I won't be able to join her. Mr. McCormack assured her he would arrange her accommodation should she visit alone.'

Hmmm, interesting. I couldn't let this one go. I couldn't let his sophisticated wife suffer the same fate as me in Henry's pokey little caravan. I promptly gave Mr. Keel a list of accomodation close to Glan Mahogue. I told him he probably shouldn't rely on Henry for that. And added that I was speaking from experience.

'Oh?' he enquired.

'I learned the hard way, that's all I'll say. Trust me. Book a hotel.'

✧ ✧ ✧

LATELY, WE'D BEEN discussing Jeffrey's upcoming live theatre performance. It was a one-off TedTalk-style information evening about makeup, skincare and fashion photography. However, now that he had 'fans', it wasn't just going to be industry folk present. Tickets were going on sale to the public and it was due to be recorded for TV. Jeffrey was working hard with his therapist on calming his nerves, perspiration and heart rate. He was stressed out in the weeks leading up to his performance. I took some time off and as ever, the grandparents were chipping in with babysitting etc.

Usually, I didn't accompany him to evening events, but this one was special and I knew how much it meant to him. He wasn't available to do my makeup, so I channelled his creativity and tried to emulate what he most likely would have done. I doubted I'd see much of Jeffrey, as I knew he'd be in demand, so my mother-in-law jumped at the chance to accompany me. She was quite the fashionista herself, easily defying the generational gap between us. We looked more like two friends, glammed up for a night out, rather than the devoted, supportive wife and mother of the main star of the night.

When we arrived, the arena was overflowing with equally, if not more glamorous ladies of all ages. I spotted Laverne and Christine, but they couldn't chat, as Jeffrey would be using them for makeup application demos on stage. The buzz was electric and I could see why this change of career presented itself as a far more exhilarating one than Jeffrey's previous, boring old IT job. It looked as though every name in the Irish fashion industry was present and I was so proud that Jeffrey's work alone could create such excitement.

We took our seats and I couldn't believe the elaborate stage before me would be his and his alone in a matter of minutes. My heart was racing for him and his mum must have sensed my nerves, so she squeezed my hand.

When he arrived on stage, I could see he was sweating already. I was hopeful that no one else would notice it, being more focussed on his charming good looks and deep knowledge of his chosen topics. Even I learned loads just by listening to him explain the fundamentals of skincare. I was all ears during the question and answer session, and wished I'd brought a notebook and pen to jot down his tips. I suppose I could watch it later, as it was being televised, or I could read all about it in the fashion mags. Then it hit me. *I'm such an idiot!* I could just ask Jeffrey, my husband! The man on stage, who we were all here to learn from...and admire.

One well-known radio broadcaster, Julie Sinclair, took the mic.

'Hi Jeffrey, it's great to be here tonight and congratulations on your success. This is a question from one of our listeners on IrelandTalks FM. What do you believe the relationship between dairy and the skin is, with a particular focus on acne? Thank you.'

She smiled and sat down. She seemed lovely, real down-to-earth. I made a mental note to tune into her radio show. Jeffrey was prepared for her question, it seemed, or else he just naturally knew all the answers. I wouldn't be surprised.

'Great question! There does seem to be a correlation between dairy, mainly cow's milk, and the severity of acne. Now I'm not a nutritionist, but I have seen the effects of going non-dairy on the skin and it can provide great relief. However, this may not be the case for everyone, so I would advise consulting your doctor before eliminating any food group from your diet.'

Then another question. I was sure I recognised the lady from the audience who asked it. She looked like my friend, Cara's, boss. Barbara, I think her name was, but how she had changed since I last met her five years ago. Tonight, she had made an effort with beautiful clothes and striking jewellery, but there was no escaping how drawn and pale and worryingly thin she looked. I guess it wasn't just Cara suffering from the pace of working in one of the country's top recruitment firms. It took its toll on all the employees. She asked an interesting question—

'Hi Jeffrey, what are your thoughts on Ayurvedic face mapping?'

'Hi, thanks for your question. Another great one! I think relating skin complaints to what's going on in the nervous system, digestive system, respiratory system et cetera is worthwhile, to say the least. Our hormones and everything we put into our bodies is linked to how our skin appears on the outside. I'm definitely interested in researching this type of face mapping more and I'd recommend it to anyone with an inclination towards it. You'll find out more about my research to date on Instagram or Twitter.'

With that, I made another mental note to sign up to Instagram and Twitter. I was only on Facebook, so antiquated now. He received one more question from the floor and I nearly fell off my chair, when I realised it was our elderly neighbour, Mrs. Johnson. If I'd known she was coming I would have offered her a lift. I should really communicate more with her and check in every now and then. She asked—

'Are expensive eye creams really worth the investment or will a good facial moisturiser work just as well?'

Jeffrey acknowledged recognition of his neighbour and she was thrilled with the attention, waving at the camera. He continued to speak about the merits of eye creams if they were applied correctly, in a gentle tapping manner, which he said he would demonstrate shortly with one of the models.

When the practical section started, Laverne and Christine took to the stage. Jeffrey took his jacket off to give his arms freer movement. I could see the sweat marks on his shirt, but only the front row would have been privy to that. I knew this would mortify him, if he thought anyone saw his perspiration, so I wouldn't mention it. If he asked me later, I'd play it down.

At the end of the evening, he received huge cheers from the audience when he informed them they could collect a makeup bag on their way out with free samples of all the products he'd used that evening. He was taken aback at the hysteria it provoked. It seemed everyone loved the idea of a goody bag.

Then, it was my turn to be taken by surprise. In his final words to the audience, he mentioned me and thanked me profusely for all my support and encouragement for him to follow his dreams. Cameras flashed in my face and I didn't know where to look. He took his final bow and caught my eye. He said something to me with that look. That smouldering look in his deep brown eyes. The look I fell in love with so many years ago. It lingered as if there was no one else in the room. I can't put words to what exactly it meant, but it was abundantly clear that the man on centre stage loved me with all his heart.

And I loved him too.

The End

Epilogue

A FEW WEEKS later, Jeffrey hammered the sign into the ground himself in a rare display of manual labour. The kids cheered and clapped when the last nail was driven in.

This would be my new, independent venture. Now that I felt ready to branch out on my own doing something I loved. Something I KNEW I was good at. The dream had been festering for a while.

It wasn't that we were falling short, money-wise. Jeffrey was killing it in the fashion world, but there were huge expenses incurred by him too. He always maintained that if he appeared successful and rich, people would treat him as though he was. This meant having the best of everything and footing the bill in order to seal the next big deal or lock in an A-list celebrity client. He knew what he was doing. I trusted his savviness. I trusted him.

As for me, I stepped back to admire this marvel of DIY performed by Jeffrey. Daniel jumped into my arms, Lauren hugged my waist and Mia was still bouncing up and down, dancing with joy.

Jeffrey took photos, professional ones with his fancy camera. I looked around. The neighbours must think the fame has gone to his head, what with a fashion shoot in his front garden.

He caught me blushing as I scanned for signs of nosey neighbours. He bent down and called Mia over. I suppose he felt a little embarrassed too in case anyone saw us. I whispered in Daniel's ear, 'I guess that's a wrap,' and started making for the front door.

'Hey, where do you think you're going?' Jeffrey called after me. I turned around and looked at him in puzzlement. He beckoned me over to the newly erected sign and reached out his arm.

'What?' I asked. 'But where's your...'

'Mia has it,' he smiled.

I gasped. 'What's Mia doing with your camera? Mia! That's Daddy's expensive work camera! Give it back!'

But Mia just laughed in my face. In fact they all did, including Jeffrey.

'C'mere,' he said. 'It's okay, I just showed her what to do. Come closer. I want one of us, together.' He was beaming now, ear to ear. 'I'm so proud of you, Beatrice.' That's when he leaned in and we kissed on the lips.

'Now, Mia!' Lauren shouted and we laughed as we heard the all important camera click.

'I got it, Daddy! I did it!' she announced. Our

lips slowly parted and we hunched down to see Mia's money shot. Tears of pride filled my eyes when I saw the image. Myself and Jeffrey, deeply connected, deeply in love, standing behind the hard oak sign he'd erected in our front garden. It read:

Abundantly Clear Communications
Private Consultancy with
Beatrice Walsh BA MA PhD Et cetera

NOTE FROM THE AUTHOR

Many thanks for taking the time to read this book. If you enjoyed it, I'd be very grateful if you would leave a review.

If you'd like to read other books from the *Midlife Secrets* series, this is Book One:
Perfectly Reasonable

To find out more about future book releases, check out my website:
www.rachelrafferty.com

And join my mailing list here:
rachelrafferty.com/newsletter

If you'd like to connect, you can reach me at
rachelraffertybooks@gmail.com

Printed in Great Britain
by Amazon